PONGWIFFY
BACK ON TRACK

PONGWIFFY
BACK ON TRACK

Kaye Umansky

Illustrated by Nick Price

First published in Great Britain in 2009 by
Bloomsbury Publishing plc
This Large Print edition published by
BBC Audiobooks 2010
by arrangement with
Bloomsbury Publishing plc

ISBN 978 1405 663977

British Library Cataloguing in Publication Data available

Printed and bound in Great Britain by
CPI Antony Rowe, Chippenham and Eastbourne

CHAPTER ONE

A TYPICAL EVENING

It was evening, and a typical scene was taking place in Number One, Dump Edge, Witchway Wood. Supper was over and Witch Pongwiffy was slumped in her armchair, eating toffees and watching Hugo, her Hamster Familiar, wash up.

The only sounds were of clinking plates and a bit of tuneless humming from Hugo and a lot of vigorous, noisy chewing from Pongwiffy.

Suddenly, the chewing stopped.

'*Gugo!*' said Pongwiffy, urgently but indistinctly. '*Gugo gy geeg!*'

Was this some sort of new language?

Hugo turned and looked at her. Pongwiffy was sitting bolt upright, pointing at her mouth with a strange expression. Sort of alarmed but sheepish at the same time.

'Vot?'

'Gy *geeg*! Gy *geeg* ga gug goo gegger!'

1

Her teeth were stuck together.

'Vot, *again*?'

'Nng.'

Pongwiffy rolled her eyes and waited for help. Hugo dried his paws on a tiny tea towel.

'It ze last time I do zis,' he warned.

He scrabbled in a drawer, took out a fork and a small hammer and advanced briskly on Pongwiffy, who quailed. With a hop and a jump, he was on her shoulder.

'Turn head,' he instructed. 'Open up.' Pongwiffy turned to face him and nervously bared her teeth. He positioned the fork and brandished the hammer. 'Ready?'

'Nng. Nnnnngggggg . . .' There was a sharp crack. '*Ah!*' Pongwiffy gave a cry as her newly freed jaws sprang open. 'Ooh, that's better. What a relief.'

'Vot I tell you 'bout eatink toffees?' scolded Hugo, clambering down.

'But they're all I've got left. I've eaten all the crunchy ones and the soft centres.'

'*Zat whole bag of sweets?* But I only got zem zis morning!'

'So?'

'Zat so greedy,' tutted Hugo. 'After great big supper too.'

Pongwiffy had indeed had a big supper. Four greasy helpings of skunk stew, no less. And now, on top of all that, she was eating sweets. Or would be, if she hadn't run out.

Hopefully, she fished around in her cardigan pocket and, with a glad little cry, produced something green, fluff-covered and frog-shaped.

'Ooh, look. A *Hoppy Jumper*.' She peered down,

2

picked off the fluff, popped it in her mouth and crunched. 'Yum. I love these, I do. I could sit here and eat 'em all night.'

'I thought you goink out,' said Hugo. 'You say you goink to visit Sharkadder.'

'Did I? Well, I'm not. I've broken friends.'

'Oh ya?' Hugo didn't sound all that surprised. Witch Sharkadder was Pongwiffy's best friend. They argued a lot, though, so they frequently weren't speaking. One day best friends, the next, worst enemies. It was hard to keep up.

'She wouldn't answer the door,' explained Pongwiffy. 'Last time I called. I know she was in there, though. Crunching sweets in the dark. Didn't want to share, I reckon. So I'm not speaking. She just doesn't know it yet.'

'So go round and tell 'er,' advised Hugo.

'How can I *tell* her if I'm not speaking?'

'Write note.'

'Can't be bothered. Too far to walk.'

'Fly zen, if you so lazy. Take Broom.'

The Broom, who had been mournfully drooping in a corner, straightened up and looked desperately keen, like a puppy who's been promised a walk. It hadn't been flown for ages and it was terribly bored, just hanging around collecting cobwebs. A brisk fly would be just what the tree doctor ordered.

'Don't want to,' said Pongwiffy. 'I want to lie around and eat sweet things. Like cake. Fetch me some cake.'

The Broom went back to mournful drooping. Hope dies quickly in Broom World, especially if you belong to Pongwiffy.

'No cake,' said Hugo. 'All gone. You eated it.'

3

'So make another one. Make a sponge cake, it'll soak up the grease. Basic science.' She gave a loud, rude belch and rubbed her stomach, which was inflated to the size of a small balloon.

'Exercise,' advised Hugo. 'Zat vot you is needink. You in bad shape.' He began poking around in the food cupboard which was empty apart from three jars of skunk stew labelled *Last Week*, *Month-Old* and *Vintage*. 'You not fit. Just lie about eatink rubbish.'

'And what's wrong with that?'

'Everysink. You should be like 'amsters. Alvays on ze go, 'amsters. 'Specially ven it comink up to ze Rodent Olympic Games.'

'The what?'

'Ze Rodent Olympics. Held in my home town, 'amsterdam. Boy, do ve train 'ard. Is big sing.'

'A big *sing*? What, like opera?'

'No, no. *Sing!*'

'Oh, *thing!*'

'Ya. Is like big Sports Day. High spot of ze year.'

'*Is* it now?' Pongwiffy gave a theatrical yawn.

'Ya. Ve play games.'

'Do you *really*?'

'Oh, ya. Rats, mice, guinea pigs, 'amsters. All join in.'

'I didn't think you got on with mice and guinea pigs. I thought you usually fought, that's what you said.'

'Not ven it ze Olympics. On zat day ve have truce. Got to be nice to each uzzer. It all about teamvork.'

'Teamwork?' sneered Pongwiffy. She didn't care for teamwork. Witches aren't known for their cooperation.

5

'Ya. Rats gotta team. Mice gotta team. 'Amsters gotta team. Everyvun compete against each uzzer, see? Ze best team vin.'

'It'd be quicker to fight, wouldn't it? Get it over and done with?'

'Not ven is *Sport*,' explained Hugo. 'Sport different. Sport got rules. Got to be fair. No fightink, no cheatink.'

'No *cheating*?' Pongwiffy sounded shocked. 'Are you serious?'

'Ya.'

'You mean—no *Magic*?'

'Certainly not.' Hugo was scandalised.

'Well, it doesn't sound like a Witch thing,' said Pongwiffy. 'Playing fair and being nice. All that effort when you can just wave a Wand.'

'Ah, but zat not ze *point*. Ze point is . . .' Hugo gave up. Pongwiffy was scrabbling through her pockets again and had stopped listening. 'Ah, never mind. Vere ze sugar?'

'How should I know? Why? Isn't there any?' asked Pongwiffy innocently, and instantly came out in green spots. (This always happens when she tells fibs. It's very inconvenient.)

'You eated it, didn't you?' said Hugo.

'I might have had a couple of handfuls, I can't remember.'

'Green spots,' said Hugo, pointing.

'All right,' said Pongwiffy sulkily. 'All right, so I did.' The green spots faded.

'You such a fibber,' said Hugo, shaking his head.

'Oh, stop lecturing me. I don't want want to be lectured by a Hamster. Leave me alone, I've got tummyache.'

'You better get better,' warned Hugo. 'Is Coven

6

Meeting midnight tonight.'

'I think I'll have to cancel. I'll send you along with a sick note. Oooooh.'

'Vot, *again*?'

'Yes, *again*. Just shut up and make cake.'

'Can't,' said Hugo. 'Run out of cake stuff. No sugar, no eggs, no flour, no nussink.'

'Well, I'm not sitting here all night with nothing to munch on. You'll just have to go along to *Sugary Candy's* and get me more sweets. I'd go myself if I didn't feel so poorly. Don't look like that, it won't hurt you. Get me a mixed bag, heavy on the *Hoppy Jumpers*. I'll have some *Bat Splatz*, and a couple of *Bog Bars*. Oh, and some *Minty Stingeroos* . . .'

CHAPTER TWO

SUGARY CANDY'S

Sugary Candy's was the name of the new sweet shop in Witchway Wood. It had only recently opened, but was already attracting a huge amount of custom. It was designed to look like a charming gingerbread cottage, with painted sweets stuck on the walls and a twist of pink candyfloss emerging from the crooked chimney. It had a pointed roof and an old-fashioned door with a quaint shop bell. But instead of poky little windows there was one great big one. The display was truly a sight to behold.

Sweets! Great big jars of them arranged in rows, all different shapes and colours. Green froggy ones, crimson ones shaped like little mouths, black bat-shaped ones that flapped in your mouth and large staring ones like eyeballs that blinked when you bit into them. There were humbugs and gobstoppers and big pink balls of bubblegum. There were huge red lollipops with faces on. There were toffees and sherbet dips and striped sticks of rock and—oh, everything under the sun. It would take far too long to describe all those sweets. You just need to know that temptation-wise, they were off the scale. They had exciting names too, written on the labels. It made them fun to buy.

As well as the giant jars of sweets, there were trays of chocolate. Big brown bars, piled high. *Slime Slabs*. *Mocklit Fudge*. *Bog Bars*.

It would have been good if *Sugary Candy's* was owned by somebody called something like Mr Twinkle or Arthur Applecheek—a merry old fellow who loved little children. It wasn't, though. It was owned by the Yeti Brothers—large, hairy, hard-headed business types who didn't love anybody.

The Yetis specialised in bad food. It was cheap and it was greasy, cooked carelessly in dirty kitchens and dumped any old how on grubby plates. Their names were Spag Yeti and Conf Yeti, and they owned a great number of greasy spoon cafes, burger bars and pizza houses in far-flung locations, all of which they ran simultaneously although nobody knew how, seeing as there were only two of them. They also did the catering for important events like parties and weddings. (Same bad food, but cut up small and served on shiny platters.) Rumour was that the Yetis cloned themselves, but it was more likely that they just ran very fast. Or took short cuts through dimensions known only to Yetis. Or possibly had a lot of identical hairy cousins with the same names.

Spag and Conf's decision to open a sweet shop was proving to be a very good one. The residents of Witchway Wood had little in common, but apparently were united in their love of lurid confectionery. *Sugary Candy's* gave them exactly what they wanted. It was pricey, mind. But, oooh. It was worth it.

Here is a typical scene. The customer can be a Skeleton, a Witch, a Banshee, a Troll, a Vampire, an anonymous hairy thing, take your pick. This is how it would go.

SPAG YETI: Yeah? What you wanna?

CUSTOMER: A large bag of *Tooth Rotters*, please. Oh, and some of your delicious *Molar Manglers*, they're my favourites. And throw in a dozen *Gloopy Guzzlers*, and fifteen of those big red lollipops and ten *Jumbo Lumpos*, the ones with the pink sprinkles. And a giant packet of *Bat Splatz*.

SPAG YETI: That-a be one month's salary, please.

CUSTOMER: *(Hands over salary)* Thank you so very much, see you tomorrow.

(Customer leaves, poor but happy. Spag rings up the till, rich and even happier.)

Business was *good*.

This particular night, Spag stood behind the counter, stuffing money into the overflowing till. There was a long queue trailing out of the door. At the front was a Werewolf, followed by two Skeletons, a family of Trolls, a small Thing in a Moonmad T-shirt, a Gnome (named GNorman, currently reading the paper), a sour-faced Tree

11

Demon and a solitary Vampire in a beret, who was licking his lips and eyeing up a jar containing the red sweets shaped like little mouths.

Three Witches stood at the back. Sludgegooey, Ratsnappy and Bendyshanks. They had come for their night's supply.

'What are you getting?' Sludgegooey asked Ratsnappy, who was breathing heavily because she had just walked up a short, gentle slope.

'Don't know yet,' gasped Ratsnappy. 'Can't talk. Still puffed out from that climb.'

'I usually have *Minty Stingeroos*, but I'll think I'll try those stripy yellow ones for a change.'

'What—*Beezi Kneezies*?' chipped in Bendyshanks, who had a swollen cheek. 'Take my advice, don't. I had those the other night. Hard as nails. Broke a tooth. I'm in agony, actually. It was a real struggle to get here. But I couldn't miss my sweet run. I'm getting *Bat Splatz*, they're softer on the gums.'

'I haven't tried those yet,' admitted Sludgegooey.

'Oh, you must!' cried Bendyshanks. 'They flap about your mouth, then explode and all this lovely green melty gooey stuff comes out.'

'Melty gooey stuff's not good for teeth, is it?' said Sludgegooey, not in a disapproving way but because she was interested.

'Takes the mind off the pain,' explained Bendyshanks.

'Oh, right. I was thinking of *Hoppy Jumpers*.' Thoughtfully, Sludgegooey eyed the rows of jars.

'Oh, don't have them,' advised Bendyshanks, the expert. 'They play havoc with the tummy, especially after a big greasy meal. And don't have those blinking eyeballs, they're horrible.'

'I hope this won't take long,' groaned Ratsnappy. 'My back's killing me from the walk up that hill. I had to lie down halfway up. Vernon had to come and give me extra special perspiration.'

'It's artificial respiration, isn't it?' asked Sludgegooey.

'All I know is I was sweating a lot.'

'I know what you mean. It's hard on the knees, walking. My knee keeps clicking. Listen.' Sludgegooey bent a knee, which dutifully clicked. 'See? I'd be tempted to bring along a chair, except I'd have to carry it.'

'You should get Filth to carry it,' said Ratsnappy.

'I would, but he's out rehearsing.'

I should explain here that Sludgegooey's Familiar is a Fiend called Filth. He is small and hairy and plays drums with the local band called the Witchway Rhythm Boys. He says 'yeah, man' a lot, even when he means 'not likely'. He is always neglecting his duties and sloping off to rehearsal. Sludgegooey puts up with this because she thinks he is creative, although she does find his habit of air drumming at the table annoying.

'You should make him,' said Bendyshanks. 'That's what you employ him for. He gets away with too much, your Filth. I'd make Steve.'

'Ah, but Steve can't *carry* a chair, though, can he?' Sludgegooey pointed out. 'It's easy to say when he can't even *do* it.'

This is true. Slithering Steve, Bendyshanks' Familiar, is a small grass snake. He has his talents, but they don't include chair carrying.

'He would if he could,' said Bendyshanks a bit

13

huffily. 'He's willing. It's hard to carry a chair without arms.'

'Some chairs have got arms,' remarked Ratsnappy, who was thinking about sweets and losing track a bit.

'We're talking about Steve's limitations,' said Sludgegooey.

'And Filth's,' added Bendyshanks firmly.

'Oh, *right*. Yes, well, all the Familiars have those, don't they? I have to admit my Vernon can be very sneaky. You have to check your change. And his cooking's terrible. I'm living on takeaways.'

'Me too,' said Sludgegooey. 'Can't be bothered to cook up a brew. Run out of herbs and whatnot. Can't go out picking, not with my clicking knee. How much *longer* is that idiot going to be?'

At the front of the queue, the Werewolf was being indecisive about his purchases. He was already weighed down with loads of paper bags full of sweets and was now wondering if he could manage a family-sized bar of fudge as well.

'Is that real chocolate?' asked the Werewolf, pointing.

'Eez-a chocolate-*flavour* chocolate,' said Spag. 'Called mocklate.'

'What's in it?'

'How should I know? I sell it, not-a make it.'

'Well, yes, but I was just wondering . . .'

'Look,' said Spag. 'You wannit? Or you donna wannit?'

'I *want* it,' explained the Werewolf. 'I just don't know if I can carry it. Do you deliver?'

'Oi!' shouted Sludgegooey. 'Get a move on, fur face, there's folks waiting.'

'There are,' said a dry voice from behind, adding

14

firmly, 'but I'm not one of them. Out of the way, coming through.'

CHAPTER THREE

SOURMUDDLE JUMPS THE QUEUE

The queue shuffled hastily to one side. This was Grandwitch Sourmuddle, Mistress of the Witchway Wood Coven, over two hundred years old, sometimes hard of hearing, often short of temper and definitely not to be crossed.

She came waddling up the line with Snoop in tow. Snoop was a small, red, officious Demon, generally considered by the other Familiars to be a bit above himself. He scampered along at her heels, bossily waving a tiny trident.

'Why is that old woman pushing in?' demanded a small Troll of his parents, who looked embarrassed and told him to shush.

Sourmuddle reached the counter and elbowed the Werewolf to one side.

'Marshmallows,' she demanded. 'The ones I always have.'

'Alla-outa, sorry. Been a run,' explained Spag, adding, 'but I gotta *Swampswallows*. Same as Marshmallows, but different colour. Orange-a.'

'What? Speak up.'

'ORANGE-A. YOU LIKE-A.'

'Excuse me?' piped up the Werewolf. 'I was here first, you know.'

'No, you weren't,' said Sourmuddle, who could hear fine when she wanted. 'Single-celled organisms were here first. They were brainier than you, though. They'd know better than to argue with *me*.' Casually, she fingered the Wand hanging from a string around her neck.

'But you jumped the queue. She did, didn't she?' The Werewolf appealed to onlookers, but was met with a lot of blank stares. Everyone was tired of his faddy ways and would be glad to see the back of him. Besides, Grandwitch Sourmuddle versus a Werewolf? No contest.

'She's allowed,' called Bendyshanks from the back. 'She's Grandwitch Sourmuddle and she can do what she likes.'

'Quite right,' agreed Sourmuddle. 'I can. Is that you, Bendyshanks? Come on up to the front, you can be next.'

'Can I bring Ratsnappy and Sludgegooey with me?'

'Are they there too? Yes, come on up, Witches go first. Anyone want to argue with that? No? Good. All right, Mr Yeti, I'll take the *Swampswallows*, but they'd better be good.'

The queue sighed resignedly as Bendyshanks, Sludgegooey and Ratsnappy pushed their way to the front, looking smug.

'Well I never!' sulked the Werewolf, then caught

18

Sourmuddle's eye and went quiet.

'I'm glad I saw you three,' went on Sourmuddle, as Spag began shaking squashy orange balls into a set of weighing scales. 'I'm changing tonight's arrangements. We're not flying to Crag Hill, we'll have the Meeting in Witchway Hall.'

The Witches always held their Meetings on Crag Hill, unless really bad weather conditions prevented it. Well, they did until the last few weeks. Up until then they flew to Crag Hill even if there were storms brewing or blizzards threatened. But lately, they hadn't been so keen. It was just such an effort, dusting the Brooms off and getting ready with the extra vest and looking for the umbrella when you could be lying around scoffing sweets in front of the spellovision. Nobody could be bothered. An excuse could always be found.

'So what's the excuse?' asked Bendyshanks. 'Is it a good one?'

'My Broom's not well. Nasty case of stiffbristle. I've got it soaking in a bucket of warm water.'

'Stiffbristle's catching, isn't it?' asked Ratsnappy, vaguely alarmed. 'I'd better check on mine. I haven't taken it out of the cupboard in ages. I heard it banging on the door a few days ago but I was in the middle of a takeaway curry and couldn't be bothered to get up.'

'You don't have to get up, though, do you? To open your Broom closet,' said Sludgegooey. 'You can just lean across from your chair.'

'I wasn't in my chair. I was in bed,' explained Ratsnappy. 'I have all my takeaways in bed.'

'So what you're saying is, you don't do any exercise at all?'

'Nope. Vernon does it for me. I make him do ten

19

press-ups every night and every morning. I feel ever so much better after watching him.'

'So why are you doing your own shopping, then?' enquired Sludgegooey.

'Oh, I wouldn't trust him with *that*. He'd come back with the wrong things. He's only a Rat, you can't let him make those kind of decisions. Especially about sweets. I like to choose my own. I'm going to have some of those *Swampswallows*, like *you*, Sourmuddle.'

'An excellent choice,' said Sourmuddle, snatching an enormous paper bag from Spag and thrusting it into Snoop's little red arms. 'Here. Don't drop 'em. I take it they're on the house, as usual?'

Spag swallowed. This went against everything he stood for. But this was Grandwitch Sourmuddle, who did as she liked.

'Yeah. I guess so.'

'Very kind, much appreciated. Now. What else do I fancy, I wonder . . . ?'

It was at this point that Hugo arrived, swinging a tiny wicker basket. He joined the back of the queue, behind the Vampire.

'Hello,' said the Vampire in hollow tones. His name was Vincent Van Ghoul, and he always wore a beret and a smock with red paint splashes because he was a bit of an artist in his spare time.

' 'Ello,' said Hugo.

'Taking a while,' said Vincent, sucking his teeth. 'Long queue.'

'Ya,' said Hugo. Hamsters and Vampires having little in common, he couldn't think of anything else to say.

'Still working for Pongwiffy, then?' asked

Vincent.

'Oh, ya.'

'Haven't seen her around lately. Nothing wrong, I hope? Stiff neck? If she's got a stiff neck, I could pop round and take a look. I'm good with necks.'

'No, no, neck not stiff. Problem is vot she put down it. Too much rubbish food.'

'She shouldn't mix colours. Tell her to eat red things. That's my advice.'

'OK.'

'Strawberries. Beetroot. Tomatoes are good.'

'OK.'

'Only red.'

'OK.'

The queue shuffled forward a bit. Sourmuddle, Snoop, Sludgegooey, Bendyshanks and Ratsnappy pushed their triumphant way back along the line, loaded down with paper bags. Sourmuddle paused and stared down at Hugo.

'Ah,' she said. 'Hugo. Where is your mistress?'

'Back in ze hovel, lyink down,' said Hugo. 'She not feelink so good.'

'Well, tell her I expect to see her at the Meeting tonight. She's missed three in a row.'

'Ya, well, she not feelink . . .'

'I don't want to hear excuses. Tell her to be there. Midnight sharp. And spread the word amongst the Familiars. All your Witches are to attend. There's been too much bunking off recently.'

'OK,' said Hugo. And the queue shuffled forward.

CHAPTER FOUR

LATE

Despite Sourmuddle's warning about punctuality, almost everyone was late to the Meeting. At midnight sharp, thirteen chairs were drawn up to the long trestle table in Witchway Hall, but only three were occupied.

Sourmuddle sat at the top end, looking grim. Arranged before her was a register, her Wand and a half empty bag of *Swampswallows*. Snoop was crouched on the back of her chair, holding a large watch and making tutting noises.

At the far end of the table sat Witches Agglebag and Bagaggle, the identical twins, with their Familiars on their laps. They were two Siamese cats called IdentiKit and CopiCat, and they were exceedingly snooty, although no one knew why as all they seemed to do was sit around posing and demanding cream. The twins had a large bag of *Bat Splatz* which they were sharing between them with a lot of rustling and whispered consultation.

'Midnight,' said Sourmuddle. 'Where is everybody?'

'Coming,' said Agglebag.

'But slowly,' added Bagaggle.

'We called in for Greymatter, but she's watching spellovision and eating chips with chocolate sauce.'

'Sharkadder's trying to hide her spots. She's had another outbreak.'

'We passed Bendyshanks coming back from the dentist.'

'And Ratsnappy, lying down halfway up the hill.'

'Scrofula and Bonidle'll be late. Scrofula's pushing Bonidle in a wheelbarrow.'

'We don't know about Macabre. Rory's refusing to let her ride. He says she's got too heavy . . .'

'Enough!' shouted Sourmuddle. 'I said midnight sharp, not breakfast time tomorrow!'

The door swung open to reveal Ratsnappy, bent double and gasping. She tottered in and flung herself into the nearest chair. She was accompanied by Vernon, who was small and sulky and looked like he'd had quite enough of doing his mistress's press-ups for her.

'Can't speak,' wheezed Ratsnappy, pulling a grubby hanky from her pocket along with a load of sweet wrappings and mopping her brow. 'Can't breathe. Got a stitch.'

She was closely followed by Bendyshanks, who had a bandage tied around her face and was groaning loudly. Then came a little group— Sludgegooey (with clicking knee), Gaga (chewing enthusiastically on a mouthful of bubblegum) and Macabre, who stood with arms akimbo and fiercely announced, 'Mutiny in the ranks! Ah had tay *walk*!

Rory refused tay carry me, can ye believe!'

All four had their Familiars with them. Bendyshanks had Slithering Steve draped around her neck. Sludgegooey had Filth, who for once wasn't rehearsing. Gaga, as always, was surrounded by a little swarm of Bats. They zoomed excitedly around her head, neatly avoiding the sticky pink bubbles she kept blowing. Macabre's Haggis, Rory, remained outside, cropping the grass and sulking. He was large, shaggy and ginger, with two sharp horns. His orange fringe hung low over his eyes. He was fed up because Macabre had just given him an earful.

'Sit down and be quick about it!' snapped Sourmuddle. 'You all get triple black marks for lateness.'

'I couldn't help it, it's my tooth,' moaned Bendyshanks.

'Anyway, we're not last,' pointed out Sludgegooey. 'Bonidle and Scrofula are still at *Sugary Candy's*. They've run out of sweets.'

'Well, they're no having any o' mine,' said Macabre, firmly patting her bulging sporran. Her chair creaked ominously as she sat down. She had put on a bit of weight recently, as Rory would tell you. Well, all the Witches had. Their tummies were very much in evidence.

'I thought it closed at midnight,' said Sourmuddle.

'It does. They're trying to break in. Well, Scrofula's throwing bricks at the window. Bonidle's snoring in the wheelbarrow. I think they'll be a while.'

'No, we won't,' said a voice. 'We're here, so there.'

25

Witch Scrofula stood in the doorway, panting heavily, holding the handles of a rickety wheelbarrow containing Bonidle and her Familiar, who was a Sloth. He didn't have a name because Bonidle couldn't be bothered to give him one. Both were snoring loudly.

'You each get triple black marks,' snapped Sourmuddle. 'No, fourple. Make a note, Snoop.'

'But I was wheeling Bonidle,' protested Scrofula.

'Fiveple black marks. For answering back.'

'No luck breaking the window, then?' enquired Sludgegooey.

'No,' sighed Scrofula. 'Waste of time, wasn't it, Barry?'

The Vulture perched on the rim of the barrow nodded sadly. This was Barry, Scrofula's Familiar. He was moulting again, and not feeling too well.

'*Ah* could have told ye that,' said Macabre. 'Magically reinforced glass, ah reckon. Tried it mahself, with a batterin' ram. *Everybody's* tried it. It's unbreakable.'

'Yes, well, we know that *now*,' snapped Scrofula crossly. She upturned the barrow and decanted Bonidle and the Sloth on to the floor. Neither woke up.

'Prop her up in a chair,' ordered Sourmuddle. 'This is a formal meeting.'

The twins jumped up and helped Scrofula hoist Bonidle into a chair. She just slumped there, with her eyes closed. Then her hand slowly rose and floated towards the twins' bag of *Bat Splatz*.

'Get off,' said Agglebag, snatching it away. 'Buy your own and stop sleep stealing.'

'So who's left to come?' enquired Sourmuddle.

'Greymatter—arrrgh! Sharkadder—arrrgh!—

and Pongwiffy,' groaned Bendyshanks, clutching her jaw. 'Arrrgh!' she added, just in case anyone was in any doubt about her pain.

'We'll start without them,' decided Sourmuddle. 'I want to get away early. My Broom's sick, I need to change its water. And I have to call in for a takeaway. We don't have time to cook, do we, Snoop? Too busy nursing poor Stumpy. Are we all ready? Hail, Witches!'

'Hail!' came the response. There came a sudden, sharp rattling on the roof as a small cloud released a barrage of hailstones before scooting off in a northerly direction. This always happens at the start of Coven Meetings.

'Right,' continued Sourmuddle. 'First things first. Whose turn was it to bring the sandwiches?'

'Greymatter's, but she isn't here,' came the chorus.

'Oh. Well, we'll start with News. Anyone got any new spells they'd care to share with us?'

There was a lot of shrugging, followed by rustling as the Witches reached for more sweets. The twins huddled over their bag, keeping a sharp eye on Bonidle. Nobody wanted to share anything, that was clear. Crazed by sugar, Gaga was swinging from the rafters, in pink bubble heaven.

'Here comes Greymatter,' said Bendyshanks. 'Don't forget to give her some black marks. Arrrgh!'

'I don't deserve black marks,' said Greymatter, marching in briskly and shaking hailstones from her hat. She had a piece of paper in one hand and a pencil was tucked behind her ear. Her Familiar— an Owl named Speks—sat on her shoulder.

'Yes, you do,' said Sourmuddle. 'You're late.'

'Ah, but that's because I was composing a poem about chips.'

Everyone looked impressed. Greymatter was the clever one. She knew a lot of long words and wrote poetry. She was good at crosswords too.

'Let's hear it, then,' said Macabre. She reached into her sporran, selected a sweet and popped it in her mouth. 'Anyone like *Porridge Balls*?'

'I do,' said Scrofula hopefully.

'Aye, they're lovely, aren't they?' said Macabre, and meanly put them away.

'Read us your poem, then, Greymatter, and we can get on with the News,' ordered Sourmuddle.

'*Ode To Chips*,' said Greymatter. 'Ahem. Chips, chips, I really love chips, more than ships, whips, parsnips, tulips, paperclips or pillowslips. Especially with dips.'

A little silence fell.

'That's not as good as your usual ones,' remarked Scrofula eventually. 'It's just a list of words with 'ips' at the end.'

'Yes, well, I haven't felt in a creative mood recently,' said Greymatter. 'You have to feel serene and settled to write poetry. My brain isn't working as well as it should be. I haven't been sleeping.'

'That's because you eat chocolate-covered chips in bed,' said Scrofula.

'You're right,' admitted Greymatter. 'I do. And very lovely they are too. By the way, I couldn't be bothered to make sandwiches, but I've brought along a bag of *Gloopy Guzzlers*. Anyone want one?'

Everyone did.

*   *   *

Witch Sharkadder came hurrying along the moonlit track that led to Witchway Hall. She was late because she had been trying to disguise the latest nasty crop of sweet-induced spots that had exploded on to her face. She had run the gamut of all her make-up, but nothing did the trick, so she had resorted to wearing a black net veil and a large pair of dark sunglasses. It wasn't a good look, particularly with her pointy hat. Her long, sharp nose stuck out, straining at the veil. It was only a matter of time before it bored a hole through.

Dead Eye Dudley, her cat Familiar, came loping along in her wake. He was large, battered and piratical-looking with one glaring yellow eye and a permanent sneer.

'Come on, Duddles,' trilled Sharkadder. 'Don't hang about. We're very late, you know.'

She rounded the bend and came across Hugo sitting on a tiny log, swinging his little legs and looking resigned.

'Oh,' said Sharkadder. 'It's you. Where's Pong?'

Hugo pointed to a nearby bush. It was shaking a bit, and there were groaning noises coming from it.

'She's turned into a bush?' enquired Sharkadder. It wasn't such an odd question. Witches often turn themselves into things, just to see what it feels like. It could be anything—a jar of pickles, an old sofa, a scarecrow, a knitted hat. A bush wasn't so strange.

'No,' said Hugo. 'She behind it. She poorly.'

He looked past Sharkadder, spotted Dudley and pulled a rude face.

'I'll scupper ye,' growled Dudley. 'I'll hoist ye from the main brace, see if I don't. By yer tiddly little *knees.*'

Hugo and Dudley didn't get on.

'Shush, Dudley, this isn't the time,' scolded Sharkadder. 'Pong? Are you all right?'

There was a pause. The bush trembled again and Pongwiffy came crawling out from behind it, looking green.

'Oh dear,' said Sharkadder. 'You *do* look rough.'

'I feel rough,' said Pongwiffy, climbing to her feet and reeling about, clutching her stomach. 'I've never felt so rough in my life.'

'Something you've eaten?'

'*Everything* I've eaten.'

'Told you,' said Hugo. 'Shouldn't have eated all zose *Hoppy Jumpers.* Told you.'

'I know you did, Hugo, and you were right. I should have listened.'

'*I* could have told you about *Hoppy Jumpers*,' said Sharkadder. 'They thump around in all the sloshy stuff you've eaten, don't they? Sort of squishing it down. Squish, splosh, sloppity squish . . .'

'Yes,' said Pongwiffy, going even greener. 'They do. But I'd like you to stop talking about it now. Why are you wearing that?' She pointed to Sharkadder's veil.

'A slight rash,' mumbled Sharkadder.

'It's worse than that, isn't it? The tip of your nose has bored through. It's covered in pimples.'

'I know,' admitted poor Sharkadder wretchedly.

'It's like a knobbly parsnip. A raw, lumpy parsnip with . . .'

'I know, I *know*. I haven't been out for a week. I've been too embarrassed to answer the door.'

'I'm aware of that. I came round. I expect you

heard me shouting.'

'Well, I'm sorry, Pong. I just didn't want anyone to see me. Even you.'

'I'm not surprised, I've never seen anything like it. That's some nose, that is. Have you been sandpapering it?'

'*No!* Look, are you coming, because we're late for the Meeting.'

'I'm coming,' said Pongwiffy grimly. 'Sick as I am, I'm coming.'

'Well, come on then.'

'You go on. I'll be there in a minute. Something I need to do . . .'

Looking green again, Pongwiffy dived behind her bush.

When she finally emerged, Hugo was still sitting on the log. He was watching something. Silhouetted against the moon, a lone squirrel was running around the branches of a tree. It twirled and leapt and swung and somersaulted, chittering happily to itself.

'See zat?' said Hugo. 'Zat vun fit squirrel. He run, he jump, plenty exercise, eat healthy nuts, 'ave fun.'

'Hugo,' said Pongwiffy, 'I have taken your point and learnt my lesson. From now on, things are going to be different. Let's get to that Meeting. And while we're walking, you can tell me all about that *thing* you were on about. The Rodent Oh Something or other. Exactly what happens . . . ?'

31

CHAPTER FIVE

PONGWIFFY'S IDEA

'I'm still waiting,' said Sourmuddle, drumming her fingers. 'Waiting for News. Come on, I'm getting irritable now. No new recipes? Anyone zapped any Goblins? Spied on any Wizards?' She broke off as Sharkadder came hurrying into the Hall with Dudley at her heels. 'Ah, there you are, Sharkadder. Sixple black marks for being late.'

'There's no such word as sixple,' pointed out Greymatter.

'There is if I say there is,' snapped Sourmuddle. 'Sixple, sevenple, twenty-twople, whatever I say.'

'I couldn't help it,' protested Sharkadder. 'I had problems getting ready.'

'That's an interesting *bee-keeping* look, Sharkadder,' remarked Sludgegooey, referring to the sunglasses and the veil. Everyone sniggered.

'Yes, well, I have a slight rash,' mumbled Sharkadder.

'That's no excuse,' said Sludgegooey. 'I've got a knee that clicks. I got here before you, though.'

'So did I, even with . . . arrrrgh! Toothache.' (That was Bendyshanks.)

'What about my back, then?' (Ratsnappy.)

'I don't think any of you realise quite how long a poem takes, particularly when one isn't in the mood . . .'

Everyone began shouting, apart from Gaga, who was experimenting to see what happens if you blow bubbles when standing on your head. (Nothing pleasant.)

'Here I am. Sorry I'm late.'

A voice came suddenly from the doorway. Everyone looked around.

'Oh,' said Sourmuddle sourly. 'It's you, Pongwiffy. A hundredple black marks for being last. Sit down, we're doing News.'

'I will,' said Pongwiffy. 'I *will* sit down, but not until I've made a very special announcement.'

'Is it News?'

'More important than News. I want you to take a good look at me.' She struck a pose. 'What do you see?'

The Witches took a good look at Pongwiffy. Some put on their spectacles. There was a little silence.

'You,' said Bendyshanks eventually.

'But a bit worse than usual,' added Sludgegooey. 'Wheezing a bit. Even dirtier, if that's possible. And smelling to high heaven, that goes without saying.'

Everyone nodded. That about summed it up.

'Ah,' said Pongwiffy. 'But what you see before you is the *Old* Pongwiffy. The *New* Pongwiffy is

about to come. Prepare for a huge change.'

There was a general sigh of disappointment.

'That's *it*?' demanded Sourmuddle. 'That's the announcement? That you're *changing* yourself? What's so special about that?'

It was pitifully easy to turn yourself into something different. All the Witches could do it, with a wave of the Wand and a muttered incantation. They could become a mermaid, a kangaroo, a steamroller, anything. Simple transformation. It wasn't the sort of thing that deserved a special announcement.

'Ah, but I'm not using *Magic*,' explained Pongwiffy. 'I'm talking about a *real* change. I'm going to do it properly. No short cuts. I took a long look at myself before I came here tonight, and I didn't like what I saw. And I can't tell you how poorly I was on the way. Hugo knows, so does Sharky.'

'She was,' agreed Sharkadder loyally. 'Poor Pong.'

'So,' announced Pongwiffy, 'I've made a decision. I'm going to get fit.'

Now, that was a word you don't hear often in Witch circles. It caused shock, bewilderment and a certain amount of rude laughter.

'You can laugh,' said Pongwiffy sternly. 'Oh, you can *laugh*. But you won't, not when you see the new me.'

'Will it have washed its cardigan?' shouted Scrofula. 'The New You?'

Everyone fell about.

'I'm not talking about surface dirt,' said Pongwiffy irritably. 'I'm not talking about *smell*. I *could*, all night long, in fact I'd love to, but I'm not.

36

I was discussing it with Hugo on the way here. He said something. What was it you said, Hugo? About treating the body as a wimple?'

'Temple,' said Hugo. 'Treat body like *temple*.'

'I think you'll find a wimple is a medieval headdress worn by . . .' began Greymatter, but Pongwiffy waved her quiet.

'Temple, wimple, pimple, whatever. The main thing is, I'm getting back on track. I'm going to start looking after myself and get healthy. I'm going to stop eating junk and go for things like—like—um—' Hugo whispered in her ear. 'Like cauliflower. And grapes.'

'That's good, is it?' asked Bendyshanks doubtfully. 'Cauliflower and grapes?'

'Certainly. Fruit, vegetables and lots of exercise.'

'All right,' said Sourmuddle suddenly. Snoop was tapping at the watch. 'That's enough of you. Let's move on to News—'

'Wait a minute, wait a minute! I haven't finished.'

'Is this a different part of the special announcement?'

'Yes.'

'Is it more interesting than the first part?'

'Yes.'

'Well, get a move on, we haven't got all night.'

Pongwiffy took a deep breath and stared around the hall. 'The thing is,' she announced sternly, 'we've *all* got to change, not just me. I've seen the light, you see. It took a lot of suffering behind bushes and an athletic squirrel, but finally I've seen it.'

'What's she on about?' sighed Scrofula. 'Bushes, lights, squirrels, what's she on about? *Can* I have

37

one of your sweets, Macabre?'

There was an instant rustle as everyone suddenly remembered their sweets. They were getting bored with Pongwiffy, who was taking far too long to get to the point.

'You see? That's just what I'm talking about!' cried Pongwiffy. 'All this rubbish we're eating! The sweets and the greasy stuff. Oh yes, it *tastes* nice, I know that, but just look at us. Tummyaches, spots, toothache. Running out of breath if we walk as far as the garden gate. Clicking knees, backache.' She whirled, pointing an accusing finger. 'Macabre's gone up three kilt sizes. Greymatter hasn't written a decent poem for weeks. We've stopped making brews. The Brooms never get taken out. Is this what the Witchway Coven has come to? A bunch of decrepit has-beens who spend all their time pigging out on *sweets*, like a load of half-baked *Gretels*?'

It was a rousing speech and there was a lot of truth in it. There came a series of guilty crunching noises as the Witches hastily disposed of the sweets in their mouths, then a hail of rustling as they tried to hide the bags. Even Sourmuddle decided against taking another *Swampswallow*.

'All we're doing,' went on Pongwiffy, 'all we're doing is making the Yetis rich and ourselves unhealthy. So it's time for a change. If I can do it, we all can. But it won't be easy, so we need something to aim for. So here's the idea. We hold a Sports Day.'

There was a long, startled silence.

'What did she say?' demanded Sourmuddle after a bit. 'Did she say—*Sport*?'

'I did. I'm speaking of a great big sporting

contest that'll be talked about for years to come. Hugo was explaining it to me. Apparently, in Hamsterdam, where he comes from, they hold something called the O'Lumpicks.'

'Not O'Lumpicks. *Olympics*,' said Hugo. 'Rodent Olympic Games, very popular. 'Amsters, rats, mice, guinea pigs, veasles, ferrets. All join in.'

'Sounds daft,' jeered Dudley. 'Load o' little furry critters running about. Daft.' Vernon gave him a glare, and he shut up.

'And the point of it?' enquired Sourmuddle.

'Well, like I said, it'll give us a goal to aim at, won't it? While we're getting fit. And not just us Witches either. We'll throw it open to all. Everyone who lives in the Wood. Skeletons, Trolls, Wizards, Vampires, Zombies, Ghouls—everyone except Goblins. We have to draw the line somewhere.'

'Why would we *do* that, though?' mused Ratsnappy. 'Throw it open to all?'

'Ah, well, you see, this is where it gets interesting. Apparently, Hugo was explaining to me, as well as making you fit, an O'Lumpicks has got a Noble Purpose.'

'*Olympics*,' said Hugo.

'The whole idea is to meet and mingle. We get to discover all the things we have in common.'

There was a bewildered silence.

'What, that we hate each other, you mean?' asked Ratsnappy eventually.

'Well . . . yes. But we pretend we don't.'

'Let me get this right,' said Scrofula slowly. 'Are you saying we have to be—*nice*?'

'Right. We have to behave in a sporting manner. No fighting.'

39

There was a rumble of disbelief. What a very novel idea. This would take some getting used to.

'I havenay got anything in common wi' a Wizard, Ah'll tell ye that,' said Macabre stoutly, to wide agreement.

(Witches and Wizards have a different style of Magic. Stinky brews versus flashy illusion. They don't mix. Witches and Wizards try to keep well apart. Although there is some intermingling. Sharkadder's nephew is a Wizard. His name is Ronald and occasionally she has him round for tea. More about Ronald later.)

'We're *Witches*,' said Ratsnappy. 'We don't *want* to mingle. Witches are superior, everyone knows that. Everyone else is riff-raff.'

There was another rumble of agreement.

'So we'll prove it,' said Pongwiffy firmly. 'We'll get fit and prove it by winning every single event.'

'Like what?'

'I dunno.' Pongwiffy waved a vague hand. 'Everything. There'll be lots of races and stuff. Running and jumping. I haven't thought it through yet. I'll have to form a Sports Committee and iron out the details.'

'Will there be prizes?' Macabre wanted to know. 'Because Ah dinnay intend tay rouse mahself unless there's a prize at the end.'

'Certainly there'll be prizes,' promised Pongwiffy rashly. 'There'll be gold medals. And silver and bronze for the runners-up. But we Witches'll be going for gold. We'll train and train until we're the fittest Coven in the world. Undisputed champions of the Witchway Wood O'Lumpick Games.'

'*Olympic*,' said Hugo.

'Why bother to train?' interjected Bendyshanks,

40

fingering her sore mouth. 'We can win everything using Magic. Simple speed spells. Strength pills. I've got a recipe for kangaroo potion at home. Three drops and I can clear the house. Not with this toothache, mind.'

'That's not *sporting*, though, is it?' said Pongwiffy. 'That's cheating.'

'Where does it say Witches can't cheat?'

There were nods of agreement all round. Witches have a very casual attitude to cheating.

'Not when it's *sport*,' said Pongwiffy. 'The whole point is to eat well and get fit. Magic doesn't come into it. Magic is banned.'

There was a shocked gasp at this.

'Ah've nivver heard such a thing!' exploded Macabre.

'There's got to be a level playing field, you see,' said Pongwiffy.

'There isn't a level playing field around here,' pointed out Ratsnappy. 'Just trees and thickets and bogs and bumpy little pathways.'

'I've thought of that,' said Pongwiffy. 'We'll use the palace gardens. We'll pull up the rose bushes and mark out a running track on the lawn. We'll have to chuck out all the old statues, of course, they'll be in the way. And maybe chop down a few trees.'

'The King won't like it,' remarked Sourmuddle thoughtfully. 'Very nice this year, his roses. Credit where credit's due, he's got a good garden.'

The King's name was King Futtout, and he did indeed have a lovely garden. He spent a lot of time in it, to stay out of the way of his wife, Queen Beryl, and their daughter, Princess Honeydimple. The palace grounds stretched right to the borders

41

of Witchway Wood and were surrounded by a high wall, to keep out undesirables.

'All in a noble cause,' said Pongwiffy airily. 'He'll agree, I'll see to that. If he doesn't, we'll do it anyway. Come on, Sourmuddle. What do you think?'

'I must say I'm struggling with the idea,' said Sourmuddle. 'It's all a bit newfangled for me.'

'You don't want to get fit, then?'

'What's the word I'm looking for?' Sourmuddle thought briefly. 'No.'

'Well, I must say, I'm shocked. You wouldn't like to run everywhere? So you could be even more punctual?'

'I'm over two hundred years old. Why run? Besides, I'm Grandwitch. It's not dignified, is it, Snoop? We don't *run*, do we?'

'Certainly not. The very idea,' snapped Snoop, breathing out a cross little puff of smoke.

'So you're saying we can't have an O'Lumpicks? You can't say we can't, you *can't*!' Pongwiffy sank to her knees and wrung her hands. 'Don't say we can't. Oh please, oh please! I'm really *keen*!'

'I haven't decided. I'm not sure about the whole mingling thing. Or the playing fair. Or the sport, come to that. But I confess that getting Futtout annoyed has a certain charm.' Sourmuddle gave a dark little chuckle. 'It's been a while since we rattled his cage.'

'It'd be very good publicity too. For the Coven, I mean.' Pongwiffy was being crafty here. Sourmuddle was never averse to good publicity. 'I mean, I know we're good at being *Witches*, everyone knows that. But this'd be something different, wouldn't it? Something that'd benefit the whole community. And we'd be the hosts, so we'd run it our way. We'd make ourselves popular and get fit and win all the gold medals at the same time. We can't lose.'

'Would I get my name in the paper, do you think?' asked Sourmuddle.

'Sure to!' promised Pongwiffy. 'You can go on spellovision too, and talk about it on all the chat shows. Just imagine it! Marching around with our flag at the Grand Opening Parade. A spectacular display of Witch pride. Traditional costumes. The band playing. Everyone cheering.'

'Opening Parade?' cut in Scrofula. Everyone perked up. It's a dull person indeed who doesn't like the idea of a parade.

'Oh yes, there has to be one of those, doesn't there, Hugo?'

'Zere does,' agreed Hugo. 'Parade first, zen Games, zen ze medals. Zat how it go.'

'All the teams march in under their own flag,' explained Pongwiffy. 'But because we're running things, we go first. So we get the biggest cheer.'

Barry the Vulture asked the question that all the Familiars were dying to ask. He wasn't feeling quite so unwell now. All the Familiars were sitting up, looking interested. Steve had wriggled out from beneath Bendyshanks' cardigan. Rory had come in from outside, and Filth had stopped air drumming. Dudley looked a bit sulky, though. Hugo was getting far too much attention in his opinion.

'Permission to speak?' asked Barry the Vulture. 'On behalf of the Familiars?'

'Go on, then, but make it quick,' said Sourmuddle. Familiars weren't encouraged to speak at Coven Meetings.

'Can *we* be a team? Instead of just running around making tea?'

There came an explosion of laughter from the Witches.

'Ah dinnay *think* so,' cried Macabre. 'The very *idea*!'

'Ha, ha, ha!' chortled Greymatter. 'Familiars competing against Witches! Oh, my splitting sides!'

Pongwiffy caught Hugo's eye.

'Yes, they can,' she shouted. 'We've got to do this right. The Games are open to all. Even Familiars.'

The laughter cut off. There was a shocked silence. Hugo whispered in her ear.

'And they can have their own flag,' announced Pongwiffy.

'I bet it's a daft one,' said Macabre, who still hadn't forgiven Rory for making her walk.

'Them's fightin' words,' growled Dudley. 'Us can make a better flag than you landlubbers, I knows that!'

'Don't be cheeky, Dudley,' Sharkadder reprimanded him. 'Just be glad Pongwiffy's given you permission. This is a Witch Meeting, you're not supposed to interrupt. What was that you were saying about traditional costumes, Pong?'

'That's what we wear before we change into our shorts. I thought you could design them, Sharky. With your good fashion sense.'

'We have tay wear *shorts*?' howled Macabre.

'Of course. A healthy diet, a noble mind, team spirit and shorts, that's what the O'Lumpicks are all about. Hey, you know what else I thought? We could get Scott Sinister to be the commentator and present the medals at the end. And you know what

44

else? We could . . .'

Hugo sat quietly on Pongwiffy's hat, listening to her rant on. A Sports Day, held in the palace grounds. A Grand Opening Parade. Races. Medals. Competition. Everyone in shorts. Everyone getting together to find out what they had in common. Scott Sinister, the famous film star, to present the prizes. It was an ambitious plan. It could be fun, or it could be a recipe for disaster.

However it worked out, one good thing had come out of it. From now on, Pongwiffy would be eating healthily. He could finally throw away those jars of mouldy skunk stew.

CHAPTER SIX

PLUGUGLY DROOLS

At exactly the same time as Pongwiffy was
outlining her big idea, Plugugly the Goblin was
standing stock-still with his nose flattened against
the window of *Sugary Candy's*. He had been there
for some time.

It was the first time that Plugugly had seen the
new sweet shop. He rarely ventured down into
Witchway Wood for fear of coming face to face
with a Witch. Goblins are sworn enemies of
Witches. Well, they're sworn enemies of everybody
actually. But they are particularly wary of Witches,
who automatically zap them on sight. (Zapping is
painful, involving a green flash, a short, sharp
scream and flaming trousers.)

However, it was the last Friday of the month,
and the Witches would be tied up with their Coven
Meeting. Plugugly had been told this by a Thing in
a Moonmad T-shirt who he happened to have

bumped into earlier, when out wandering the mountains with his empty hunting bag.

Usually, Plugugly hunted with the rest of the Gaggle. A Gaggle, you should know, consists of seven Goblins who do everything together—eat, fight, and sit around plotting stupid things mainly. But on this particular evening, Plugugly was alone. This was because he'd had a big argument with the others. It had been about hats. More specifically, whose hat was best. Like all Goblin arguments, it had come to nothing, but the general agreement seemed to be that out of all their hats, Plugugly's was the silliest.

Plugugly was fond of his headgear, which was an old saucepan he'd found in a dump. He thought it was a bit helmet-like and made him look like a knight of old. It didn't. It just made him look like a Goblin with a saucepan on his head.

Anyway, it all ended with him seizing his hunting bag and stomping out in a fury.

'Ow!' the Thing in the Moonmad T-shirt had said, picking himself up. 'Watch where you're going!'

'I is in a *hurry*,' Plugugly had snapped. 'I is goin' *huntin'*.' He waved his bag, which had the Traditional hole in the bottom. (Goblins always persist in cutting that Traditional hole, although they sometimes wonder why they never succeed in catching anything. It is one of their stupidest Traditions, although they have others that come close.)

'Why? It's not Tuesday.'

(This is another Tradition. Goblins always hunt on a Tuesday. Everyone knows this, including the prey, which is why they never catch anything and

48

live on stinging nettle soup.)

'It isn't?' said Plugugly doubtfully. He had no calendar and relied on his fingers to count. He often got it wrong.

'No,' scoffed the Thing. 'It's *Friday*. The last Friday of the month. The Witches' Coven Night. Don't you know *anything*?'

'I know I'll bash you up,' said Plugugly crossly.

'Oh, oh, I'm so scared!' jeered the Thing, and went skipping off, leaving Plugugly to reflect upon his words.

So. It was the last Friday of the month. The Witches would be tied up with their Meeting. That meant there would be no Witches wandering around the Wood, although he'd need to keep an eye out for Trolls. Worth the risk? Probably.

Plugugly made for the Wood. He knew he wouldn't catch anything with a *face*, because he never did. Faces tend to have brains behind them. Even really tiny brains belonging to small, dim mice are more than capable of outwitting a Goblin.

But, reckoned Plugugly, there might be toadstools. Or, if he was lucky, some of those red berries you could add to nettle stew. They made it look pretty, although you always felt funny afterwards. Anyway, whatever he got, he would take it back to the cave and scoff it in front of everyone. Without sharing. That'd learn 'em.

The moon was out and the sky was splattered with stars, so it wasn't too dark under the trees. Nevertheless, Plugugly kept his saucepan pulled well down over his eyes to protect him from low branches. Of course, that meant he couldn't actually *see* them, so his passage through the woods was accompanied by a series of loud ringing noises. *Clang! Ping! Dong!* You could hear him coming a mile away. Lots of little fluffy things sat smugly in their holes, nudging each other and sniggering.

Plugugly hadn't ventured down into the Wood for some time, so he was very surprised when he came across *Sugary Candy's*, sitting slap bang in the middle of a glade. More than surprised. Goblinsmacked. That's the same as being gobsmacked, but worse, as you will see.

Dazzling light blazed from the window of the beautiful gingerbread house, the glistening sweets shining like jewels in the moonlight. The window was chock-a-block with big, multicoloured jars and mountains of heaped chocolate bars. The shop might be closed, but Spag and Conf knew the value of advertising their wares twenty-four seven and always left the shutters open and the lights on.

Slowly, Plugugly pushed back his saucepan so that he could get a proper eyeful.

Plugugly had only ever eaten sweets once in his life. On one never-to-be-forgotten occasion, the Gaggle had attended a fancy dress party at the Great Gobbo's palace. They had eaten wonderful things there. Jellies. Cakes. Pink wobbly stuff. Brown sticky stuff. Best of all, handfuls of delectable sweets from deep bowls. Oh my, what a night that had been.

The shop window drew Plugugly like a magnet. His feet left the ground, and before he knew it he was standing with his nose glued to the glass, mouth open and drooling, well and truly goblinsmacked.

That was how the Gnome called GNorman

found him.

'What are you doing there, Plugugly?' enquired GNorman. He was on his way home to supper, a copy of *The Daily Miracle* tucked under his arm.

Plugugly didn't even look round.

'Oi! You!' shouted GNorman. 'Plugugly! What are you doing?'

Plugugly gave a faint moan and continued to drool.

'No point in looking,' said GNorman. 'They're closed.'

Slowly, Plugugly dragged his eyes away. He turned. His eyes were glazed and his mouth hung open. He was slavering really badly.

'Sweeeteeeeeeez,' drooled Plugugly.

'Yes, I know,' said GNorman impatiently.

'Sweeeeeteeeeeeeezzzzzzz . . .'

'That's right, sweets, that's what they sell.'

'Sweeeeeeeeeeeeeeeeeeee . . .'

Plugugly was obviously stuck in a groove. His brains were jammed. GNorman picked up a fallen branch and hit him on the saucepan very hard.

CLAAAANG!

'Ow,' said Plugugly crossly. 'Dat hurt.'

'Had to be done,' said GNorman. 'You should thank me. I asked you what you're doing here in the Wood, where you're not supposed to be?'

'Nothin'. Just lookin'.'

'There's no point. They're closed. The door's got a magic padlock on it. And you can't break the window, if that's what you're thinking. Everyone's tried, it's hopeless.'

'Bet I can,' said Plugugly.

'Go on then. Let's see you do it.'

Plugugly marched back some way from the shop,

lowered his head and ran full tilt at the window. He collided with it, rebounded and fell flat on his back.

BOING!

'See?' said GNorman. 'Not even a little crack.'

'But I want *sweeeeeties,*' moaned Plugugly. He sat up, clutched his head and rocked to and fro. 'I *want* dem. I do, I do, I *do*!'

'Well, you'll have to pay for them like everyone else,' said GNorman. 'Come back when they're open, and bring lots of money.'

'But I hasn't got no money!'

'So get a job and earn some.'

'What job?'

'I don't know, do I? Look in the paper.'

'But I can't *read* de paper.'

'How pathetic,' sighed GNorman. 'I don't know, can't even read the paper. You Goblins are *hopeless . . .*'

His voice suddenly cut off. That was because Plugugly's hand was around his neck.

*   *   *

Plugugly's Gaggle lived in a damp cave on the lower slopes of the Misty Mountains known as Goblin Territory. Their names were Hog, Lardo, Slopbucket, Stinkwart, Eyesore and Sproggit. They didn't like living where they did—it was a desolate place, full of rocks, rain and rubbish. But sadly, they were stuck there. A long time ago they had fallen foul of a Wizard who had banished them there for ever as a punishment, so there wasn't anything they could do about it. No matter how far they hiked, in the end they always ended up back

52

in the cave, so they never bothered going far.

They were sitting around in sullen silence, wishing there was something to eat, when the boulder that served as a front door came crashing back and Plugugly burst in and announced, with great triumph, '*I has got a Gnome!*'

He had too. Poor little GNorman was tucked tightly under his arm, legs wiggling.

'Can we eat it?' asked Eyesore hopefully.

'*You* can eat it,' said Plugugly, adding, 'Dat's up to you. But *I* isn't. *I* is goin' to eat . . . *sweeeeeteeeez*!'

There was a united gasp. Sweeties? What was this?

'Where you gonna get sweeties from?' enquired Hog. 'There ain't no sweetie trees round 'ere last time I looked.'

'Ah,' said Plugugly, 'I know. But I has seen somethin' very excitin'! Dere's a new shop! Down in de Wood! Dere's lots o' sweeties! Big jars of 'em! Like what we had at de Great Gobbo's party dat time, but *better*! I saw dem!'

'Liar,' said Stinkwart. 'There ain't no sweet shop in the Wood.'

'Dere is!' insisted Plugugly. 'If you doesn't believe me, ask *him*.'

He set GNorman on a small rock. The rest of the Gaggle crowded round.

'Look what you've done to my paper,' said GNorman crossly, trying to straighten out the creases. 'Do you have to be so *rough*?'

'Tell dem,' said Plugugly, giving him a poke. 'Tell dem about de new shop.'

'All right, all *right*. There's a new shop. It's called *Sugary Candy's*. The Yetis own it. It sells overpriced sweets. Can I go now?'

'Oh no,' said Plugugly. 'You isn't goin' nowhere. I has got plans for you.'

'What?' asked GNorman, a bit alarmed. 'You can't eat me, I don't taste nice.'

'Niver does nettle soup, but we eats that,' remarked Slopbucket.

'We isn't eatin' de Gnome,' said Plugugly firmly. 'Dat's not de plan.'

'What is, then?' piped up Lardo.

'Ah,' said Plugugly. All eyes were upon him. He was enjoying the attention. 'Ah. Well, see, I bin finkin'. Dere's dis sweetie shop, right? An' we likes sweeties, right? So I was finkin' we can get some money, see, and den—*we can go to de new shop an' buy some*!'

'Oh yeah?' That was young Sproggit, sounding highly sarcastic. 'Oh *yeah*? And where we gonna get money from? Livin' round 'ere? Ain't no *banks* to rob, is there? 'Cept mud banks!'

Everyone howled with laughter at the thought of a bank in Goblin Territory.

'I know *dat*,' said Plugugly. 'I know dere isn't no banks. And dere isn't no buried treasure an' nobody never gives us no pocket money. And nobody's nan's due for a visit. So dat only leaves one fing. We has got to get a job.'

A silence fell.

'A job?' said Eyesore after a bit. 'You mean— like, *work*?'

'Dat's right,' said Plugugly. 'We does a job an' dey gives us money. Dat's how it works, right, Gnome?'

'What job?' asked Eyesore.

'Ah. Dat's where de Gnome comes in.'

54

Everyone stared at GNorman.

'He's already in,' observed Stinkwart. 'You brought him, under yer arm, just now.'

'No, no. I know he's *in*. He's in de *cave*, I know dat. What I mean is, he can read out de jobs in de paper.'

'I don't see why I should,' snapped GNorman. 'I'm not a reading machine, you know. You can't put a penny in the slot and make me read.'

'We can poke you wiv a sharp stick and make you blub like a *babby* though,' said Lardo, and everyone sniggered.

'Ain't no banks to rob round 'ere,' said young Sproggit, in the hopes of regaining the comedy crown, but his time was gone and he was ignored.

'Go on, Gnome,' said Plugugly.

'That's what I'd *like*,' said GNorman. 'I'd *like* to *go on 'ome*.'

Everybody else was trying to be funny, so he thought he might as well. Sadly, his little play on words fell on stony ground. Goblin humour is very basic. Witty Gnomish puns go over their heads. The sort of thing that makes a Goblin laugh is someone falling over a cliff.

'Get readin',' said Plugugly. 'Or else.'

GNorman sighed. It seemed there was no getting out of it. He sat down cross-legged, took a pair of spectacles from his pocket, hooked the ends around his pointy ears and said firmly, '*Sit*. You have to sit when you're being read to.'

Obediently, the Goblins sat. GNorman opened the paper to the Situations Vacant page. The Goblins watched his every move. This reading business was a complete mystery to them. They were in awe.

'Right,' said GNorman. 'Here goes. TREE FELLERS WANTED. APPLY AT WOOD YARD.'

'Dat's no good,' said Plugugly. 'Dey only want tree, an' dere's seven of us. What else?'

'MILKMAIDS WANTED. IF COLD HANDS, DO NOT APPLY.'

'None of us are called Hans,' remarked Slopbucket. 'Does that mean we can apply?'

'None of us are milkmaids, though,' said Stinkwart doubtfully.

'Funny name for a milkmaid, ain't it? Hans?' reflected Hog. 'They're usually called Betty.'

GNorman was getting tired of all this.

'It's *Cold Hands*! Not called Hans. They want milkmaids with hands that are *not cold*.'

'Not called what?' said Hog, confused.

'Anyway,' said Plugugly, 'anyway, we is not girls an' cows doesn't like us. Carry on.'

'GARDENERS WANTED AT PALACE. APPLY KING FUTTOUT.'

'We ain't workin' for King Futtout,' cried Lardo. 'Remember when he chased us outa his orchard that time? Like them apples *belonged* to 'im, or summink?'

'They did,' pointed out Stinkwart. 'It was his orchard.'

'Oh yeah,' said Lardo. 'I see what you mean.'

'Carry on,' said Plugugly to GNorman. 'We isn't gardenin' for royalty, dey doesn't like us. What else?'

'VAMPIRE WANTS HEADLESS HORSE-MAN. MUST HAVE FULL COACH DRIVING LICENCE.'

'Nope. Can't drive coaches, got heads, and

56

Vampires . . .'

'Don't like you, yes, I thought that might be the case,' said GNorman wearily, adding, 'You're being very fussy, you know.'

'Go on,' insisted Plugugly. 'What else?'

'Not much. This is the last one. WANTED. LIVE-IN NANNY FOR NEW BABY BOY. APPLY MR AND MRS STONKING, STONKING TOWERS. BIG BAG OF GOLD FOR THE RIGHT PERSON.'

There was a long silence. After a bit, Sproggit asked what they were all thinking, 'What's all that about then?'

CHAPTER SEVEN

THE STONKINGS

The Goblins know nothing about the Stonkings. Not being privy to the gossip grapevine in Witchway Wood, they are never up to date with the news. It will be down to GNorman to bring them up to speed.

It is the following day. Right now, the Stonkings are sitting on the stout reinforced balcony of their big flashy house. The house sits atop a hill overlooking Witchway Wood. In the distance are the Misty Mountains. They have an enviable view. Down below, there is a big garden with big sunshades, a big ornamental fountain and a big barbecue with an ox-spit. There is also a garage containing a great, big, shiny red motorbike because the Stonkings are keen bikers.

They are also Giants. Did I mention that?

Bigsy Stonking has his shirt off and is enjoying the rays of morning sun, which glint off the gold medallions nestling in his chest hair, the gold rings on his fingers, the gold chains around his wrists, the gold hoops in his ears and the single, big gold ring through his nose.

His wife, Largette, is wearing a heavily stained pink bathrobe and a massive pair of sunglasses. She has her hair in curlers and is painting her toenails red. It would be an idyllic scene if it weren't for the sound of angry roaring coming from somewhere inside.

'THIS IS THE LIFE, EH, PETAL?' thundered Bigsy. Giant speech has to be written in capital letters, because it is VERY LOUD.

'IT WOULD BE,' agreed Largette, 'IF BABY PHILPOT WOULD JUST GIVE IT A REST FOR TWO MINUTES. TALK ABOUT STRESS. LOOK AT THE MESS I'M MAKING OF MY NAILS.'

'RELAX, PETAL. STICK COTTON WOOL IN YER EARS. I DO.'

'I'VE GOT NO TIME TO MYSELF AT ALL. I LIKE TO LOOK NICE, BIGSY.'

'I KNOW YOU DO, PETAL.'

'I HAVEN'T EVEN HAD TIME TO TAKE MY CURLERS OUT.'

'I KNOW, I KNOW.'

'LISTEN TO HIM, BIGSY. HE NEVER STOPS. HE WANTS FEEDING AGAIN.'

I should explain that the Stonkings have only just moved into this very large, flashy remote house. The house has to be large, flashy and remote for these reasons:

1. They are Giants.
2. They are seriously rich and can afford to throw

their money around.
3. They have a brand new baby boy who does nothing but ROAR.

Let me tell you a bit about Giants in general. Never confuse Giants with Ogres. They are quite different. Bigsy and Largette Stonking do not have two heads. Well, they do, but not two *each*. They do not rampage around in seven league boots, waving clubs with nails in. They don't kick down mountains or juggle sheep. They're not *that* big, or that bothered. Even if they were, they wouldn't have found the time, not with the new baby, who is very demanding.

No, Ogres they are not. But that isn't to say they aren't big. I mean, *really* big. To put it into perspective, you would probably come up to Bigsy's knee. The Stonkings would have trouble fitting into your house. Unless you live in a cathedral.

Most Giants live somewhere they call The Big Country, a long way from Witchway Wood. There is only one town in The Big Country. Predictably, it is called Giant Town. Almost all Giants live there, mainly because it has a Giant supermarket called Vasto's which always has special offers.

Giants tend not to travel much. This is because everything in The Big Country is the right size for them—big. Nowhere else in the world caters for them properly. Everywhere is too small and everything is horribly fiddly. There are very few houses they can comfortably fit in. Only really rich Giants settle elsewhere, mainly because they *can*. They can afford to have new, big furniture made and get big food imported from home.

Bigsy Stonking can afford it. He has plenty of cash to throw around. His family owns Vasto's.

To tell the truth, there was another reason why the Stonkings moved, apart from wanting to show off. Neither of them liked their mothers-in-law. Largette didn't like Bigsy's mother, and Bigsy didn't like Largette's. Neither of the mothers liked their son-in-law, daughter-in-law or each other, so it was all very fraught at family barbecues. This is how it went, when they talked about moving.

* * *

Largette: I'M TELLING YOU NOW, I'M NOT HAVING YOUR MUM INTERFERING, BIGSY. NOT WHEN OUR BABY ARRIVES. SHE WAS BAD ENOUGH AT OUR WEDDING.

Bigsy: I KNOW, PETAL, I KNOW.

Largette: SHE WAS RUDE ABOUT MUM'S HAT.

Bigsy: I KNOW. (A pause.) YOUR MUM WAS RUDE ABOUT 'ERS FIRST, THOUGH.

Largette: THAT'S BECAUSE IT WAS HORRIBLE. ANYWAY, I'M NOT HAVING HER COMING ROUND BEING BOSSY AND TELLING US WHAT TO DO. I WANT TO MOVE FAR AWAY, BIGSY. I WANT A BIG HOUSE ON TOP OF A HILL. SOMEWHERE QUIET. JUST US, WITH A NURSERY FOR OUR NEW BABY.

Bigsy: AND YOU SHALL 'AVE ONE,
           PETAL. BIGSY'LL BUY YOU ONE.

He was as good as his word. He purchased the big
house on top of the hill, bought big flash furniture
and big flash sunshades and the barbecue and
everything they needed to make life comfortable.
And then Baby Philpot arrived.

The Stonkings weren't prepared for Philpot.

You should know something about Giant babies.
When they are first born, they are surprisingly
small. Bigger than a human baby, of course, but
still quite small. Their lungs are big, though, so
they roar really loudly. They do this for three
weeks. That's all they do—roar, drink milk,
eliminate milk and roar again. They never sleep.

Baby Philpot was just like all Giant babies—
angry. He never, *ever* stopped roaring. Not ever.
He was permanently purple in the face. He never
smiled. He never slept. Just roared.

He was doing it now.

'IT'S YOUR TURN TO GIVE HIM HIS
MILK,' said Largette. 'MY NAILS ARE STILL
WET.'

'IN A MINUTE,' said Bigsy.

'WELL, GO ON THEN.'

'I WILL, I WILL. IT'S JUST THAT 'E NEVER
SEEMS TO *WANT* IT.'

'HE'S A BABY, BIGSY. HE'S GOT TO HAVE
MILK, IT SAYS SO IN THE BABY MANUAL.
NOTHING BUT MILK FOR THE FIRST
THREE WEEKS. THREE BUCKETS A DAY,
THAT'S WHAT HE'S SUPPOSED TO HAVE.'

'BUT HE SPITS IT BACK IN YER FACE! I
CAN'T GET IT DOWN 'IM.'

'WELL, YOU'LL HAVE TO TRY. IT'S YOUR TURN,' said Largette crossly.

'YEAH, YEAH, ALL RIGHT.'

'GO ON THEN.'

'I'M GOING, I'M GOING.'

'PUT HIM IN HIS PRAM, TAKE HIM FOR A WALK. HE MIGHT NOD OFF.'

'OH YEAH. SINCE WHEN HAS HE NODDED OFF?'

'NEVER,' admitted Largette with a sigh. There was a heavy silence.

'BIGSY?' said Largette.

'WHAT?'

'I'M TIRED OF BABY PHILPOT. DOES THAT MAKE ME A BAD MOTHER?'

'WELL—YEAH,' said Bigsy. 'BUT THAT'S NORMAL, AIN'T IT? DON'T BEAT YERSELF UP.'

He was right. Giants don't make the best parents. Well, not for the first three weeks, when their babies are small, sleepless and permanently furious.

But that stage only lasts for three weeks, thank goodness. When Giant babies are exactly three weeks old, they produce their first tooth and immediately go on to solids. (That means food that you can chew as opposed to drink.) They stop roaring then, and just eat. They eat continuously, and that makes them grow. And I mean *grow*. They become walking, talking toddlers in a matter of days. Then they thump about and say cute things and become much more agreeable. Their parents start liking them then.

'I JUST HOPE THERE'S A GOOD RESPONSE TO THE ADVERT,' went on

Largette.

'THERE WILL BE, YOU'LL SEE.'

'BECAUSE I NEED HELP, BIGSY. I CAN'T DO IT ALL.'

'I KNOW, PETAL. AND YOU WON'T 'AVE TO, NOT WHEN YOU GOT THE NANNY.'

Bigsy stuffed cotton wool back in his ears, closed his eyes and thought wistfully about the big, flashy red motorbike that he never got to ride now he was a father. Largette gave a little sniff, and despondently eyed her toenails.

Inside the house, the baby roared.

CHAPTER EIGHT

THE SPORTS COMMITTEE

'Right,' said Pongwiffy briskly. 'Let's get started. You fetch the fungus sponge, Sharky, and somebody put the kettle on.'

It was the first meeting of the Sports Committee. There were eight of them squashed around the table in Sharkadder's kitchen—four Witches and four Familiars. Pongwiffy, Sharkadder, Greymatter and Macabre accompanied by Hugo, Dudley, Speks and Rory, who stood outside with his head through the window.

'I didn't make a sponge,' said Sharkadder. 'We're not supposed to be eating cake, are we? If we're getting fit?'

'You didn't make a *sponge*?' Pongwiffy was aghast. Sharkadder's fungus sponge was famed far and wide for its delectable deliciousness.

'No. But there's good news. I have prepared a delicious bowl of healthy fruit and vegetables, which we can nibble on.'

'What sort of fruit and vegetables?'

'Sliced lemons tossed with sprouts.'

'Mmm,' said Pongwiffy. 'Well, maybe later, if we're desperate. Ready with your pen, Greymatter? You have to write everything down. Write Witchway Wood O' Lumpick Games in big black letters.'

'*Olympic*,' said Hugo tiredly.

'First, we've got to write down a list of what games we're having. There's got to be a running game, a jumping game, a game where you throw things, a game where you lift things and a relay race at the end. Write it down. Now, moving on . . .'

'Wait a minute there!' That was Macabre, who had only got on the Sports Committee because she threatened Pongwiffy with violence. 'Ye cannay decide just like that!'

'Yes, we can,' argued Pongwiffy. 'We're the experts here, me and Hugo. Hugo's *done* a Sports Day. He's done a whole O'Lumpick, haven't you, Hugo?'

'*Olympic.*'

'Stop correcting me, I like O'Lumpick better. Anyway, that's what you do on a Sports Day. Run, jump, throw things . . .'

'I have a question about running, Pong,' said Sharkadder, sticking her hand up. 'Where do we run? In a circle? In a straight line? Over a cliff? Do we all run at the same time? If we trip up, can we start again? Where do we stop? Who says? How do we know? Does everyone have to wear shorts? Can we wear high heels if we like?'

'That's a hundred questions,' said Pongwiffy

irritably. 'We'll be here all day and all night if we ask a hundred questions about everything. This meeting is just to get things started. We'll sort out the details later.'

'Bad idea,' argued Greymatter, who was frantically scribbling away with her tongue out. 'Sharkadder's quite right. We have to do things properly right from the start.'

'No, we don't,' insisted Pongwiffy. 'All we need right now is a broad plan of action. Details are boring, details can wait.'

'No, they *can't* . . .'

Let's just break off a minute and examine the Sports Committee while they're arguing.

Pongwiffy and Hugo had enjoyed selecting the Sports Committee. They had held auditions, and asked everyone to make a small speech about why they wanted to be on it. Everyone was keen, apart from Sourmuddle who announced that they could do what they liked as long as she got her picture in the paper.

Everyone else turned up to audition. Some of the speeches were rather good, and it's a shame we don't have time to hear them. In the end, Pongwiffy chose Sharkadder because she was her best friend, Greymatter for her writing skills, and Macabre because she had to (the threat of violence, remember?). The ones who weren't chosen—Gaga, Ratsnappy, Bendyshanks, Sludgegooey, Scrofula, Bonidle and the twins— were terribly disappointed and more than a little resentful, but there was little they could do but trail off home and wait to be told what would happen next.

'Look,' said Pongwiffy. 'It's my idea and we're

doing things my way.'

'Ah'll tell ye what we're gonnay do,' said Macabre, whose blood was up. She thumped the table with her fist. 'We're gonnay write doon suggestions. We're all gonnay ha' a say, that's fair. Like, Ah want Tossin' the Caber.'

'And what is that?' enquired Pongwiffy through politely gritted teeth.

'It's where ye take a Caber an' toss it.'

'And what is a *Caber*? Can we buy one? Do you know of any *Caber* shops?'

'Ah think a sharpened tree'll do the trick. Write it doon, Greymatter.'

'You know, I rather like the idea of the Egg and Spoon,' observed Greymatter, pausing in her scribbling. 'It's a jolly sort of race, isn't it? All that tripping up and losing your egg. It's hilarious. I mean, this is the O'Lumpick *Games*. Games implies enjoyment. It's meant to be fun.'

'I thought Sport was meant to be taken seriously,' remarked Sharkadder.

'So it'll be a funny Egg and Spoon Race which we take seriously.'

'Fair enough,' said Pongwiffy, who quite liked the idea of a seriously funny Egg and Spoon Race. 'Write it down.'

'Don't forget Veightlifting,' put in Hugo. He flexed his little furry muscles. 'I sink I vin zat, no contest.'

Across the table, Dudley exploded into helpless laughter.

'Don't be rude, Dudley,' Sharkadder reprimanded him. 'He's a guest in our house.'

'Shouldn't there be a Sack Race?' enquired Speks.

71

'There has to be a High Jump . . .'

'And what about a Three-Legged Race? There has to be one of those . . .'

Everyone was shouting at the top of their voices at once.

'All right, all right, that's enough!' shouted Pongwiffy. 'Caber Tossing, Egg and Spoon, Sack Race, Three-Legged, Weightlifting, High Jump and Relay. That's seven Games. Should be plenty, there won't be time for any more.'

'How will it work, though?' mused Greymatter. 'Everybody can't enter for everything. It'd be chaos.'

'Explain, Hugo,' said Pongwiffy vaguely. She wasn't sure herself how it would work.

'Is simple,' explained Hugo. 'Vun from each team enter each event.'

'So how do we decide who does what?' persisted Greymatter, who had a tidy mind and liked to get things straight. 'In the Witches' team, I mean? Suppose everyone wants to be in the same thing?'

'We'll get Sourmuddle to make a ruling,' said Pongwiffy. 'Everybody has to go along with her decision. That's fair, isn't it?'

'Nobody else had better Toss the Caber, that's all Ah know,' said Macabre. 'Ah thought of it and Ah'm tossin' it. Or things'll get nasty.'

'No, they won't,' said Pongwiffy sternly. 'Nastiness doesn't go with the spirit of the O'Lumpicks. We're a team. We have to support each other and pretend we don't care, even if we do. Now, let's move on. We've got to think about publicity. Hugo and I thought of asking Vincent Van Ghoul to do some posters.'

'I don't know,' demurred Greymatter. 'All that

red. Does it give the right message, do you think? It's a Sports Day, not a gore fest on a battlefield.'

'He's cheap, though,' pointed out Pongwiffy. She was right. He was. 'I'll pop along and see him tomorrow.'

'What about telling the King we're holding it in his garden?' enquired Sharkadder. 'Who's doing that?'

'I am,' said Pongwiffy. 'I'll go along after I've seen Vincent.'

'I've just thought of something,' said Sharkadder. 'Who'll be the judge?'

'Hmm.' Pongwiffy frowned. She hadn't thought about that.

'Got to have judge,' chipped in Hugo firmly. 'Say who vin vot.'

'He means who wins what,' translated Pongwiffy.

'Ya. Zat vot I *say*.'

'No, you didn't,' sneered Dudley. 'You can't talk proper, we all knows that.' Sharkadder gave him a sharp tap on the tail, and he subsided.

'He's right, though,' went on Pongwiffy. 'Come on, everyone, think. Who's going to be the judge? Although, actually, *I* wouldn't mind. Perhaps I'll compete and be a judge as well. Then I'll be certain to get a gold medal.'

'You can't do zat,' chipped in Hugo. 'Zat not sporting. Has to be somebody who not *in* it.'

'Sourmuddle could be the judge,' suggested Sharkadder. 'Then all of us Witches will get gold medals.'

Hugo gave a heavy sigh.

'No,' he said wearily. 'Look, I keep *tellink* you . . .'

'We know, we know,' interrupted Pongwiffy. 'It's

73

got to be fair, we know. It's just that it takes a bit of getting used to. Like eating greens instead of cake.'

'Talking of that, *do* have a delicious lemon sprout,' said Sharkadder. There was a little pause while she passed them round. Everybody took one. Even Dudley, who was a cat and didn't like them. Rory took two. The Familiars were taking the healthy eating thing as seriously as anybody.

'So who do we get to judge?' said Pongwiffy, crunching noisily.

'Vot about ze King?' piped up Hugo. 'He not competink, right? Give him sumpsink to do.'

'Hugo,' said Pongwiffy, 'you are a little genius. Futtout can be the judge. He'll be thrilled. Right, I think that's everything for now. I shall visit Scott to tell him he'll be commentating and giving out the medals. I expect I'll be gone some time. We're old friends, Scott and me, he's sure to offer me refreshments. I expect I'll get something to eat at the palace too. Cake with royal icing, I expect.' Hugo gave her a little poke. 'Oh. Right. Sorry, forgot. Got to be healthy. I'll order salad.'

'You, you, it's all aboot you,' complained Macabre. 'What are the rest of us doing while you're off visiting artists and kings and film stars?'

'Greymatter can write out the list of Games. And design the entry forms. We'll need lots of those, we're sure to have millions of competitors. And she can hammer out the rules too, as she's so keen on detail. And contact *The Daily Miracle* and the spellovision people.'

'What about me?' asked Sharkadder. 'I want an important job, because I'm your best friend, remember.'

'You can start designing the costumes for the Grand Parade. And you can come up with the team flag, Macabre.'

'Suppose Ah don't want tay do the flag?' protested Macabre. 'Suppose Ah want tay do something else?'

'Tough. You wanted to be on this committee, so commit.'

'Ah'll give you *commitment*! Ah'll commit mah fist to your *nose* . . .'

'Anyone for another sprout?' put in Sharkadder brightly.

Nobody was.

CHAPTER NINE

NANNY PLUGUGLY

The Goblins sat in a circle in the cave, surveying the results of their latest hunting trip. Well, let's be clear. Not so much a hunting trip as a *stealing* trip. It had taken them all day, but now they were back with their spoils.

The spoils consisted of six items. These were: a large blue spotty frock (stolen by Lardo from a washing line); a straw bonnet with flowers on it (snatched from a little old lady's head by Sproggit); a white starched apron (snipped by Eyesore from the waist of a tearful milkmaid); a wicker basket (wrenched from the hand of a small girl by the gallant Slopbucket); a big glass medicine bottle with a screw top (found by Hog in a skip); and lastly, a stick.

The stick was Stinkwart's contribution. He hadn't been paying attention when GNorman was explaining what a nanny should have in order to look like a nanny. He had wandered around in a daze all day and finally decided on a stick rather than come back with nothing.

'You done good,' said Plugugly approvingly. 'It's all good. 'Cept for the stick.'

Stinkwart looked mutinous and muttered something.

'Wot?' said Plugugly. 'Wot did you say?'

'He said wot's wrong with a stick,' interpreted Sproggit.

'Everythin',' said Plugugly firmly. 'Nannies don't have sticks. Did de Gnome say anythin' about nannies havin' sticks? No.'

Stinkwart muttered something else.

'Wot?'

'He said the Gnome didn't say nuffin' about them *not* 'avin' sticks,' said Sproggit.

'He didn't say nuffin' about dem not 'avin' *tractors*, or—or *telescopes*, or—or—or—*accordions*, did 'e?' cried Plugugly. 'That's daft, that is. We gotta fink about wot nannies *do* 'ave, dat makes 'em nannyish. A frock, an apron, a bonnet, a basket an' a big bottle o' baby medicine, dat's wot de Gnome said. Not a *stick*. It'd frighten de little baby, walkin' in wavin' a great big *stick*.'

'Ah, shut up,' said Stinkwart, and went into a deep sulk.

'The thing is,' said Lardo suddenly, 'the thing *is*, we can't *all* be nannies, can we? We ain't got enough nanny fings.'

'You're right, Lardo,' agreed Plugugly. 'Dere's only one of everythin'. Dat means only one of us can be de nanny. An' you know wot? I fink it should be me.'

'I don't see why,' growled Stinkwart. 'You didn't

78

get none o' the nanny stuff.'

'Dat's 'cos I was gettin' rid of de *Gnome*,' cried Plugugly. 'I 'ad to take de *Gnome* back, didn't I? I done more dan my fair share! I found de sweetie shop. Anyway—' his eye fell on the voluminous blue spotted frock, 'anyway, I fink dat frock'll fit me best. I fink it's my size.'

'You don't know that,' said Stinkwart.

'Yes, I do.'

'Try it on, then.'

'I will,' said Plugugly. 'Shut yer eyes. No peekin' 'til I say.'

Everyone obediently closed their eyes. There followed several minutes of rustling noises. Then . . .

'All right,' said Plugugly. 'You can look now.'

Six pairs of Goblin eyes opened—and six Goblin jaws hit the floor.

'Oooooooh,' breathed Hog. 'Get *you*, Plug!'

Plugugly was transformed. The frock fitted him perfectly. So did the flowery bonnet, tied under his chin with a large bow. The apron gave him a motherly, capable air, and the basket added a charming touch.

' 'Ow do I look?' simpered Plugugly, and patted his bonnet.

'I 'ardly knows you wivvout yer saucepan,' admitted Lardo.

'I 'ave to say the bonnet suits you,' agreed Eyesore. 'An' the dress is your colour an' all.'

'Really?' Plugugly swished his skirt. He wished he had a mirror.

'You can't just *look* like a nanny, though,' remarked Stinkwart, still put out about the poor reception of his stick. 'You gotta *talk* like a nanny.

Bet you can't do that.'

'Why, you rude, *naughty* little boy!' trilled Plugugly in a falsetto voice. 'Anudder word from you, and I is puttin' you straight to bed widdout any supper!'

The Goblins cracked up at this. They rolled around the floor, clutching their stomachs and sobbing with mirth, all except Stinkwart. It was so funny, hearing Plugugly talk like that.

'Say somethin' else, Plug!' begged Sproggit. 'Go on, say somethin' else!'

'All good children got to wash der hands before teatime!' Plugugly advised them, and was rewarded with another blast of merriment. It wasn't often he got the chance to shine.

'Do anuvver one, Plug!' urged Hog, wiping his eyes.

Plugugly reached into his basket, pulled out the big glass bottle and waved it around.

'Line up an' take your medicine like good little children!' Vigorously, he shook the bottle and waited for more laughter. There was a bit, but not much.

'Come along, come along!' he tried again. 'Everybody in line!'

Silence.

'That's not so good,' said Stinkwart. 'The bottle don't slosh. You can tell there's nuffin' in it.'

'Dat's right,' said Plugugly. 'It is empty. I know dat. But it won't be on de day. We'll fill it wiv baby medicine.'

'We ain't got any medicine,' pointed out Lardo.

'So we'll use pretend medicine. Like—like—' Plugugly cast his eyes around, looking for inspiration. They fell upon the rusty bucket of nettle soup by the front boulder. It contained the Goblins' food for the day. 'Like nettle soup.'

'Pretend medicine won't *work*, though, will it?' said Stinkwart triumphantly. 'They'll know you're not a real nanny if the medicine don't work. They'll know that right away. Think you're so clever. Givin' out pretend medicine, ha.'

'It might work,' said Plugugly crossly. Stinkwart was really getting on his nerves.

'No, it won't.'

'Well, dat's all you know, Stinkwart. You fink nannies 'ave big *sticks*. You don't know nuffin' about nuffin'. Anyway, I'm de nanny an' I know best, so shut up.'

'You needs a name,' observed Lardo. 'Whatcha gonna call yerself?'

Plugugly reflected. It was a good point. He needed a lady name. A nannyish name. Nanny Plugugly didn't have the right ring.

'I fink,' he said finally, a bit shyly, 'I *fink* I would make a good Susan.'

The Goblins considered this.

'Try it,' advised Lardo. 'We'll tell you. Go on, be Susan.'

'Good mornin',' trilled Plugugly, and dropped a little curtsey. 'I is Nanny Susan an' I has come to look after your little babby. Is dat de dear little feller? Wot a beauty. I do believe he has your eyes. Pass 'im to me, 'e needs windin'.'

The Goblins stared in amazement.

'Cor!' said Hog. 'That's good, that is. 'Ow d'you know all this stuff, Plug?'

'I dunno,' said Plugugly. He was as surprised as the rest of them. 'Seems to come natural, like. I musta bin a nanny in unudder life.'

81

'Well, that's it, then,' said Lardo. 'Plug'll be the nanny. And the rest of us can take it easy an' wait for 'im to bring 'ome the bag o' gold.'

'Suits me,' snarled Stinkwart. ' 'Long as 'e's not in the cave, suits me.'

Plugugly lost his temper then, and there was a bit of a fight.

CHAPTER TEN

THREE VISITS

Pongwiffy had three visits lined up, so she took the Broom. It hadn't been flown for ages and it went a bit mad. Both she and Hugo were decidedly windblown when they arrived at the red-spattered studio of Vincent Van Ghoul.

Convincing Vincent to provide the posters was easy. Pongwiffy had hardly started outlining the idea before he was racing around excitedly, laying out brushes and jars of red paint and outlining his creative vision.

'I thought perhaps—um—you might use another colour?' ventured Pongwiffy. 'Like, one that isn't red? Just for a change?'

'I am an artist,' said Vincent stiffly. 'I *think* you can leave the artistic decisions to me.'

He seemed a bit put out, so Pongwiffy didn't stay to argue. She had a busy day ahead. Next stop, royalty.

King Futtout was in his shed, admiring his lovely gardens through the small window. He had a kettle brewing on a small stove. The heady scent of cut grass wafted in. He'd been out mowing his velvet lawn all morning, and was sitting down for a well-earned rest.

The King liked it in his shed. He had got it kitted out very comfortably, with an old throne, a tin of custard creams, a bowl of home-grown tomatoes and a pile of old *What Coach?* magazines. He spent all his spare time there, mainly to get away from his wife and daughter who both nagged him a lot. Futtout was a small, weak, droopy sort of king, who wasn't very good at standing up for himself. Sometimes his loving family even followed him down to the shed and stood over him while he wrote out large cheques.

Not this morning, though. This morning they had gone shopping, and a peaceful time lay ahead. Or so he thought.

The door crashed open and, to his horror, a Witch came marching in, bringing with her a very familiar smell that instantly filled the shed, quite cancelling out the scent of grass. On her hat sat a small Hamster, casually polishing its nails.

'Oh,' mumbled King Futtout miserably. 'It's you, Pongwiffy.'

It should be mentioned here that King Futtout has had dealings with Pongwiffy in the past. There had been a nasty kidnapping incident involving her, the Hamster and Princess Honeydimple. Ankles had been bitten. Hair had been hacked. Harsh words had been exchanged. It had cost him money. He remembered it well.

'I want a word with you, Futtout,' announced

Pongwiffy. 'They said I'd find you skulking down here.'

'Erm?' bleated King Futtout plaintively. 'Erm . . . quite what . . . ? What can I . . . ? Erm . . . do you have an appointment?'

'Nah,' said Pongwiffy breezily. 'Witches don't need appointments. Mind out the way, I need to sit down. Oooh. Tomatoes. I'll have one of them.'

She pushed past King Futtout, helped herself to a tomato and threw herself into the old throne. King Futtout eyed her uneasily. He never got visits from Witches unless they wanted something.

'So,' said Pongwiffy cheerily, biting into the tomato. A squirt of juice shot out, narrowly missing his eye. 'How's the kinging going? Keeping you busy, are they?'

'Well, yes. I do have . . . erm . . . royal things to be getting on with,' said King Futtout nervously.

'Well, this won't take long. I've just come from Vincent Van Ghoul and I'm on my way to Scott Sinister, so I won't hang about. I just popped in to tell you that we're having a Sports Day called an O'Lumpicks and we need a big, flat space to hold it in.'

'*Stadium,*' said Hugo.

'That's right, stadium. And the only place is your garden, Futtout.'

King Futtout's jaw dropped. A *Sports Day*? In his *garden*?

'We'll need to shift a few things,' went on Pongwiffy. 'The rose bushes will have to go for a start, and the statues. Oh, and we'll need somewhere to store our costumes and flag for the Grand Opening Parade.' Her eyes flicked around the shed. 'This'll do, when it's cleared out.'

'Impossible!' The King's voice came out in a high-pitched little squeak. 'I really cannot agree to this. This is taking things too far. The gardens are private property, you know.'

'And very nice they are too. Which is why you won't want an invasion of purple-toothed snails. Or big, mad space moles. Or Ninja locusts.'

Pongwiffy withdrew her Wand from her pocket and fingered it thoughtfully. The colour drained from King Futtout's face.

'You wouldn't,' he said.

'You know I would,' said Pongwiffy cheerfully, adding, 'But I won't need to, will I? You won't want it getting round that the King refuses to support a fun-filled sporting event that will benefit all the community. Besides, it's all arranged. The posters'll be up on the trees tomorrow. And *The Daily Miracle*'s doing a piece.'

'When?' croaked King Futtout, through numb lips. 'When is this—event—to be?'

'In three weeks' time. Everyone's got to get into training and there's all kinds of things to organise. You'll have plenty of time to get the shed cleared out. We'll send a party of Familiars to start chopping stuff down and marking up the lawn nearer the time.' Pongwiffy stood up. 'Well, that's it. I'm off. I've got a film star to visit. Nice tomato, by the way. I'll take a couple more for the journey. Oh, one last thing. You're the judge. So you'll need to come up with some medals.'

'Medals?'

'Yep. Gold, silver and bronze. We'll need loads, so I'd get cracking on that.'

And with that, she was off, leaving poor King Futtout stunned.

'I hope you noticed I didn't take any biscuits,' remarked Pongwiffy to Hugo, as they flew over the trees. 'That's because I'm starting to eat well. I think it's making a difference, you know. I'm already feeling a lot perkier than I was.'

They had been flying for quite some time. They were heading for Scott Sinister's holiday retreat—a rather smart castle that lay on the other side of Witchway Wood. It was surrounded by a high wall to keep out intruders. However, it had a big iron gate with bars, through which the curious could catch a glimpse of the blue, coffin-shaped swimming pool which took up most of the courtyard.

This is probably a good moment to tell you a few things about Scott Sinister. Scott is a rich, famous star of stage and screen. He has appeared in a great many horror films, including *The Rampaging Mummy*, in which he played the evil daddy, and *Return of the Avenging Killer Poodles*, which broke box office records. He has an on/off girlfriend called Lulu Lamarre, who Pongwiffy loathes. His career took a nasty dip at one point, but now he is back on top of his game, with a new film in the offing and a lucrative job on spellovision, advertising dental products. He is currently enjoying a short rest before filming starts. He is greatly adored by Pongwiffy, who cuts out pictures of him from magazines and drags him into any of her schemes that require a celebrity. He doesn't enjoy her attentions, but knows better than to turn her down. She is, after all, his number one fan—

and number one fans should never be crossed, especially if they are Witches.

So there you have it. That's Scott. And his peace is about to be shattered.

He was lying in his purple silk hammock by the side of the pool. On a small table, set within easy reach, was a bottle of champagne, a single glass and a large bunch of grapes. His eyes were closed and he was just on the brink of a nice little snooze, when a dry voice said, 'So sorry to disturb you, sir. You have a visitor, I'm afraid.'

The voice belonged to the butler, a tall Skeleton in a tailcoat whose name, strangely, was Tubbs.

'Wha— ?' said Scott, struggling to open his eyes against the sun.

'He said you've got a visitor,' chirped a second voice. A shadow fell across his face, and he became aware of a horribly familiar smell. 'Surprise! Wakey-wakey, Scott, it's meeee!'

Scott fumbled for his sunglasses, set them on his nose and struggled upright, hoping it was a nightmare. It wasn't, though.

'Oh,' he said heavily. 'Pongwiffy.'

'Got it in one!'

There she was, beaming down at him. As always, her wretched Hamster sat on her hat.

'I knew you'd be pleased,' she went on. 'Thought I'd drop by. Just a social call. Have a little chat. Any chance of a cuppa?' She stared pointedly at Tubbs, who was hovering disapprovingly in the background, folding up towels and straightening grapes.

'I'm just about to go out,' lied Scott. 'I have an appointment with my director.'

'Good job I caught you, then. It's milk, five

88

sugars.' Hugo gave a little cough. 'No, actually, skip the sugar. And the milk. And the tea. I'll have a large mug of hot water, shaken not stirred. Got to think about the new me. Off you go, butler, Mr Sinister and I have things to discuss.'

'We do?' groaned Scott as Tubbs stalked off into the castle.

'We do. I've got a small favour to ask.'

'You have?'

'Yes. We're organising a big Sports Day, here in Witchway Wood. Everybody'll be joining in, it's very inclusive. We're calling it the O'Lumpick Games and we need you to do the commentating and give out the medals at the end. Oh, and you won't get paid because it's a Noble Cause.'

'It is?'

'Oh, yes. Everybody's going to be on their best behaviour, because it's Sport. There won't be any fighting. So, that's all sorted.'

'Look,' said Scott desperately. 'Look, I'm really busy, I'm not sure I can fit it in.'

'Oh, I think you *can*, you know,' said Pongwiffy mildly, helping herself to grapes.

'I don't think you quite understand . . .'

'No.' Pongwiffy cut him off. '*You* don't understand. This is a great opportunity. This is *big*. There'll be crowds from far and wide. It's going to be spellovised. The world will be watching. And there you'll be, in close-up, doing what you do best. Think of the exposure!'

Scott thought about this. Publicity was certainly a good thing. And filming wouldn't be starting for another few weeks.

'You're sure it won't end up with a fight?' he said.

89

'Certainly not. The very idea. Have some of Scott's grapes, Hugo, they're lovely.'

'It's just that things involving you usually do.'

'Ah, but this is Sport. It's different.'

She was right. It was.

Scott gave in.

CHAPTER ELEVEN

PLUGUGLY GETS A JOB

Plugugly stood gasping on the top doorstep of Stonking Towers. It was the biggest house he had ever seen. He glanced back at the distant gates, which seemed miles away. The rest of the Gaggle were back there, where he'd left them. He couldn't see them, but he knew they would be watching. It was up to him now.

Plugugly patted his bonnet and straightened his apron, staring up at the mighty front door. He felt nervous. Not only was everything really big, but there was a terrible roaring noise coming from somewhere within. It sounded like a wild animal. Maybe a lion, or one of those big grey wrinkled things with hosepipe noses. What were they called? Plugugly didn't know.

There was a huge brass knocker hanging above his head. He had to stand on tiptoe to reach it.

BOY-OY-OY-OY-OING!

The echoing crash made his ears ring. There was a short pause, then the sound of approaching footsteps. *Loud* footsteps. The huge door opened—and Plugugly found himself face to face with his first ever Giantess.

Actually, it was more face to knee. The Giantess's face loomed over him from a great height. She wore a grubby pink dressing gown and fluffy pink slippers. Her hair was in curlers and there were bags under her eyes. Her lipstick looked like it had been applied during an earthquake. By the looks of her, she hadn't been sleeping well.

'YES?' boomed the Giantess from on high. 'CAN I HELP YOU?'

It was all rather unsettling, but it has to be said that Plugugly rose to the occasion. A vision flashed into his head of him and the rest of the Gaggle sitting in the cave surrounded by sweet mountains. He had to keep his nerve and hold on to the dream.

'Good mornin',' he trilled in his nanny voice. He bobbed a little curtsey. 'I is Nanny Susan an' I has come about de job.'

He wasn't prepared for the Giantess's reaction. Her eyes widened and she gave a gasp of excitement.

'BIGSY!' she bellowed over her shoulder. 'GET DOWN HERE RIGHT NOW! WE'VE GOT ONE!'

An answering distant bellow came from somewhere inside. Plugugly couldn't make out the words, though, because of that awful background roaring. Whatever could it be?

'You mean—I got de job?' asked Plugugly. He

92

didn't think it would be *that* easy.

'OF COURSE'. The Giantess turned back to him. Her big face was wreathed in smiles. 'YOU DO *LIKE* BABIES, DON'T YOU?'

'Oh yes,' said Plugugly. 'Oh yes, I likes dem. Dat's cos I is a nanny. I has got de clothes an' de basket an' everyfin'.'

'SO I SEE.'

'Know what else I got?'

'WELL—NO. DO TELL ME.'

'Medicine,' said Plugugly proudly. He took the bottle from his apron pocket and gave it a vigorous shake. Liquid sloshed about inside.

The Goblins had made a real effort with the pretend medicine. It consisted of nettle soup with crushed berries to give it a nice pink colour and a few handfuls of mud to thicken it up.

'MY WORD,' said the Giantess, clearly impressed. 'YOU *ARE* PREPARED. WELL, *DO* COME IN, NANNY SUSAN. COME AND MEET MY HUSBAND, HE'S UP SEEING TO THE BABY.'

'Ah,' nodded Plugugly understandingly. 'Tryin' ter get it to sleep, eh? Must be difficult, wiv dat 'orrible noise goin' on. Wot *is* dat noise, by de way?'

'AH,' said the Giantess. Her smile wobbled and she bit her lip. 'AH. NOW, I THOUGHT YOU MIGHT MENTION THAT . . .'

*   *   *

Time now to meet Baby Philpot. We've heard him quite a bit, but haven't yet seen him in the flesh. Prepare yourself.

93

The Stonkings had thrown money at Philpot's nursery. It was right at the top of the house. It was painted blue, with a border of charging elephants that matched the curtains. Big, clanking mobiles hung from the ceiling, mostly rhinos, hippos and other large, galumphing animals. Arranged on shelves was a huge collection of soft toys—again, following the big animal theme.

Philpot's crib was in the middle of the room. It was large and lovely, all draped in blue. It had ribbons and frills and was set on wooden rockers specially designed to gently lull the baby to sleep. It was the most expensive crib in the Giant Baby Catalogue—probably the whole world. It was a shame that it didn't come with a money back guarantee, because it certainly wasn't having any effect on Philpot.

Right now, it was shuddering violently and crashing to and fro on its rockers like a ship in a storm at sea. Its inmate was beside himself.

Baby Philpot was purple in the face. Drenched with sweat. Arms flailing, back arched. Eyes screwed up, hands clenched into fists. Mouth a gummy red O, and enough noise issuing from it to unplug drains.

Lying in the corner was a gigantic baby bottle, leaking milk on to the floor. Philpot had just hurled it at his father in a fit of pique. All around the cot lay the evidence of his unsettled state of mind—a torn blanket, a gnawed pillow and a cuddly gorilla with a chunk out of its leg.

Now, you know about Giant babies. You know that they are appalling for the first three weeks, when they do nothing but roar, vomit, thrash their arms and go purple. You know that they never ever

95

sleep, as sleep would be a waste of good thrashing and roaring time. What you don't know is why. This is why.

They hate milk!

Yes. That is why Giant babies are so miserable. Milk disagrees with them. They don't like the taste and it gives them tummyache. So they sick it up, which means that they are always ravenously hungry. If only people would stop feeding them milk, they'd be just fine. But grown-up Giants can be a bit slow and haven't worked that out. By the time the babies have developed enough basic speech to explain the problem, they've forgotten they ever had it, so the traditional way of feeding babies—with milk—carries on to the next generation.

It would be funny if it wasn't so sad.

So there was Philpot, bellowing his hatred of milk to the world. Bigsy was cowering by the door, fingering a lump on his head and flinching at the barrage of sound.

The nursery door opened, and in came Largette, followed by Plugugly.

'THERE HE IS,' said Largette, pointing. 'THAT'S PHILPOT. OUR SON. THIS IS NANNY SUSAN, BIGSY. SHE'S COME ABOUT THE JOB.'

'Oh my,' said Plugugly. 'Dat is one unhappy baby. Someone should pick him up.'

'THEY SHOULD,' agreed Largette, not moving.

'DON'T LOOK AT ME,' said Bigsy. 'LITTLE SO-AND-SO JUST CHUCKED 'IS BOTTLE AT ME.'

Neither of them seemed keen. Both of them

96

were casting hopeful sideways glances at the new nanny. This was the moment, then. The moment that Plugugly needed to demonstrate his credentials.

He picked up his skirts and marched to the crib. He stood on tiptoe, and peered over.

'RRRRRRRRRAAAAAARRRRRrrrrr . . . ?'

The roar trailed off as Baby Philpot suddenly registered a new face in baby world. A face he had never seen before. It wasn't a beautiful face, but it had a big, bulbous nose and was topped with a funny hat with pretty flowers. This was different. Who was this stranger staring down at him? Philpot said, 'GA?'

'Aaaah,' said Plugugly. 'Wot a fine big feller. I do believe he has your eyes. Dere, dere, never fear, Nanny's here.'

'I'M AFRAID HE CAN BE A BIT OF A HANDFUL,' admitted Largette. 'LIKE I SAY, HE ROARS ALL THE TIME. WE DON'T KNOW WHY, THOUGH, DO WE, BIGSY?'

'NOT A CLUE,' admitted Bigsy. 'PERHAPS NANNY SUSAN CAN TELL US?'

Plugugly didn't have a clue either. But it wouldn't do to say so. He was supposed to be an expert. Why did babies cry? He cast around for inspiration. His eyes alighted on the gigantic baby bottle.

'What is you feedin' him?' asked Plugugly.

'MILK,' said Largette firmly. 'NOTHING BUT MILK FOR THE FIRST THREE WEEKS. UNTIL HE CUTS HIS FIRST TOOTH.'

'SO WHAT D'YOU THINK, NANNY SUSAN?' rumbled Bigsy. 'WHY'S HE CRYIN'?'

'I is finkin' he has got de tummyache,'

97

announced Plugugly. It was the only thing that came into his head.

'REALLY?' Bigsy turned to Largette. 'HEAR THAT, PETAL? NANNY SUSAN THINKS PHILPOT'S GOT TUMMYACHE.'

'I does,' agreed Plugugly. 'But dat's all right, 'cos I has got dis baby medicine.'

With a flourish, he produced the bottle. He gave it a proper businesslike shake. The contents sloshed about, making a very satisfactory noise. Then Plugugly began unscrewing the cap. The Stonkings watched in fascination. So did Philpot. For a moment. Then he lost interest and opened his mouth to roar again.

'HAVE YOU GOT A MEASURING SPOON?' enquired Largette.

'No,' admitted Plugugly. *Darn!* A spoon. He hadn't thought of that. Was he about to be rumbled?

'SO HOW DO YOU KNOW HOW MUCH TO GIVE HIM?'

'He's a big baby,' said Plugugly. 'So he is needin' a big dose.'

And with no more ado, he crossed his fingers for luck and upended the bottle into Philpot's gaping mouth.

The roar that had just been about to burst forth turned into a choke as the mixture of crushed berries, boiled stinging nettles, rust and mud swilled into Philpot's mouth and spilled over, running down the sides and soaking the mattress. There was such a lot of it, he was forced to swallow.

And then—a miracle happened. To everyone's amazement, Philpot licked his lips. A big, goofy smile spread across his moon-like face. His fists unclenched and slowly, his purple cheeks faded to pale pink.

'GA,' said Philpot approvingly.

'OH MY,' gasped Largette. 'SEE THAT, BIGSY? HE'S *SMILING*! THE MEDICINE'S MADE HIM *BETTER*!'

He was—and it had! Nobody was more surprised than Plugugly. From now on, he must trust his nanny instincts. They were *good*.

'WELL, LOOK AT THAT!' marvelled Bigsy. 'SHE PUT 'ER FINGER RIGHT ON THE PROBLEM.'

'Yes,' said Plugugly. 'I did. Now, I fink you should go away and leave him to me. We needs to bond.'

'OH,' said Largette. 'ALL RIGHT. SHOULD WE VISIT?'

'Not too often,' said Plugugly firmly. 'Just leave 'im to me. It's best. I'm de nanny now.'

CHAPTER TWELVE

INTERESTING NEWS

'Well, strike me sideways with great big green balls of fire!' spluttered Dave the Druid, dropping his fork with a clatter. Half a sausage rolled across the table and landed in the lap of Gerald the Just, who looked annoyed.

'Is that a *request*, or something you've seen in the paper?' enquired Frank the Foreteller, helping himself to a dollop of mustard.

'I don't believe it! They've come up with some batty ideas, but this one takes the cake!'

'Who have?' asked a disembodied voice from an empty chair. This was Alf the Invisible, who preferred to take his reversing pills after eating.

'The Witches. Shush, I'm reading.'

The Wizards were in the dining room of the Clubhouse, eating breakfast. Breakfast mostly consisted of greasy sausages, and plenty of them. There was bacon and eggs and black pudding as

101

well, but greasy sausages were the most popular, followed by endless rounds of toast and jam, all washed down with copious amounts of sugary tea.

There were seven Wizards, and six had beards. (You'll have to take my word about Alf the Invisible's beard. I know you can't see it right now, but I assure you he has one.) The only Wizard without the traditional chin shrubbery was Sharkadder's nephew, Ronald the Magnificent. He was trying very hard to grow one, but never quite managed it. Being the youngest and least important, he sat at the far end of the table near the door, in the draught.

'I don't see why you should have the paper,' said Fred the Flameraiser irritably. 'It's always you who reads it first.'

'That's because I'm the one who goes all the way down to the front door and picks it up off the mat,' explained Dave the Druid. 'I *bend down* to get it, don't I?'

'That seems reasonable to me,' said Gerald the Just. 'Dave makes the effort, so it's only fair he should read it first.'

'Well, at leasht read ush out a bit,' piped up the Venerable Harold the Hoodwinker, dunking a sausage into his tea. He was the oldest Wizard and liked his food soggy, because his teeth were missing. 'What doesh it shay about Witchesh?'

'They're organising some sort of *sporting* contest.'

'Sport?' exclaimed Frank the Foreteller. 'You mean—*running around*?'

'That sort of thing,' nodded Dave the Druid. 'The O'Lumpick Games, they're calling it. Open to everybody. They're to be held in the palace grounds. They're inviting teams to apply. All welcome, it says.'

'Good grief!' scoffed Frank the Foreteller, spooning jam on to his toast. 'What a thoroughly unpleasant idea.'

'Just imagine,' said Fred the Flameraiser, who had shredded up his napkin, made a little pile on his plate and was now in the process of setting fire to it with a candle. 'Running around Futtout's garden with a load of common riff-raff.'

'Quite sho,' nodded the Venerable Harold, dunking a fried egg. 'Why would one want to *do* that, I wonder?'

'It says here to get fit,' said Dave the Druid. 'And to intermingle.'

A chorus of braying chortles greeted this. Fitness wasn't high on the Wizards' agenda. The only exercise they got was shuffling between the table and the armchair. Apart from Dave the Druid, who had a daily bend down to pick up *The Daily Miracle*, and Ronald the Magnificent, who always did the weekly sweet run down to *Sugary Candy's*. As for intermingling—well! That was beyond the pale.

'It says that there are medals to be won,' added Dave. 'And it's going to be spellovised.'

'Good,' said Alf the Invisible. 'We can sit and watch in our armchairs and sneer. It's ridiculous, and we're certainly not getting involved.'

And then a lone voice piped up from the far end of the table.

'Oh, I don't know,' said Ronald. 'It might be . . . fun?'

There fell a heavy silence. It was the pause before the storm.

'*Fun?*' Frank the Foreteller thundered. 'What has *fun* to do with Wizardry? Are you *mad*? What d'you think, everyone? Is he *mad*? *I* think he's mad . . .'

Poor Ronald. He gets severely picked on at this point, and it's quite painful. It only stops when Dave the Druid starts reading out an advertisement for a new type of sweet called *Wizard Wobblers*. And then only because they want him to go and get some.

*   *   *

All over Witchway Wood, the various factions were opening *The Daily Miracle* and reading about the proposed O'Lumpick Games.

It should be explained here that the Wood is home to a wide variety of clans. Witches, Skeletons, Trolls, Zombies, Banshees, Gnomes, Fiends, Bogeymen, Vampires, Ghosts, Ghouls— they all live there, keeping themselves to themselves, doing their own thing and only mixing under duress. As well as the main clans, a number of odd individuals live there too. The Thing in the Moonmad T-shirt; a bad-tempered Tree Demon; a couple of bandaged Mummies called Xotindis and Xstufitu; the Werewolf from the sweet shop queue—it's amazing how heavily populated the Wood is. Of course, being a magical sort of place, it manages to accommodate everybody who chooses to live there whilst still remaining essentially wood-like. Quite how this works is a mystery. But it does.

Of all the reactions to the news, none was quite so volatile as that displayed at King Futtout's breakfast table. Queen Beryl was the first to read the headlines, because she insisted on having the paper first.

'Futtout!' she snapped, causing her husband to choke on his Kingios.

'Yes, dearest?' bleated King Futtout, as soon as he recovered his breath.

'What is *this* I am reading on the front page?'

'Urm—I really don't know, dearest. Something interesting, is it?'

'Have you consented to something called the *O'Lumpick Games* to be held in the palace grounds? Without consulting *me*?'

'Ah,' quavered King Futtout. 'Ah. I was going to mention that.'

'I want more ithe-cream,' announced Princess Honeydimple suddenly. She spoke with an annoying put-on lisp. She sat between her parents on a little golden chair with a pink cushion. She had long, curly yellow hair and big blue eyes. She wore a white frilly frock and white satin slippers. She was horribly spoiled and allowed to eat ice-cream for breakfast, which, as everybody knows, is not a good thing.

'In a moment, darling,' said Queen Beryl. 'I'm talking to your father. Explain yourself, Futtout.'

'It happened while you were out,' twittered poor Futtout. 'I wasn't expecting her, she just barged into the shed, you see, and . . .'

'*Who* barged into the shed?'

'Erm. Her. You know. The Witch. Pongwiffy.'

'Oh, *poo*!' snarled Princess Honeydimple. '*Her! Thee* cut my *hair* off!'

Honeydimple was telling the truth. Pongwiffy had indeed cut off a hank of her hair. She had needed princess hair as a vital ingredient for a spell. It had happened some time ago, but Honeydimple was the type to bear grudges.

'What,' thundered Queen Beryl, 'were you *thinking* of, Futtout? Entertaining that appalling creature in your shed? After what she and that *dreadful* Hamster did to Honeydimple?'

'Yeth,' chipped in Honeydimple. 'How *could* you, Daddy?'

'I wasn't entertaining her, she just came in making demands and *threatening* me . . .'

'Threatening you? How did she threaten you, pray?'

'She was talking about—about purple space snails and—erm—ginger locusts. She took her Wand out, you see, I had no choice in the matter . . .'

'You are the King!' roared Queen Beryl. 'Kings always have a choice. I will not *have* it, Futtout. I will not *have* that mad woman commandeering the palace gardens for some dreadful *sporting* event. Even if she is a Witch!'

'That'th right,' chipped in Honeydimple. 'You tell him, Mummy.'

'I'm afraid I don't see how we can stop her, dearest. She was very insistent . . .'

'*Nonsense!* You will write immediately and tell her you've changed your mind. The very idea!'

'But—'

'You heard me.'

'But—'

'Straight after breakfast, Futtout. You will get pen and paper and write her a very stiff letter which I will dictate. And that will be the end of the matter.'

106

So King Futtout wrote a stiff letter to Pongwiffy, which Queen Beryl dictated. He put it in an envelope, stamped it with the royal seal and affixed to it a first-class stamp.

He didn't post it, though.

CHAPTER THIRTEEN

MINDING THE BABY

'Dere, dere,' crooned Plugugly, bending over the crib. 'Oo's a good little baby, den? Oo's Nanny's treasure-poo?'

Philpot waggled his chunky arms and kicked his fat, dimpled legs. He was beaming. Plugugly reached in and tickled his fat, pink tummy. Philpot thrashed about in delight, giggling.

'*Oo's* a little sugar plum? *Oo's* Nanny's lovely boy? Baby Philpot, dat's who! Dat's *you*, dat is.'

'TEE HEE!' laughed Philpot, clearly loving it. 'TEE HEE!' And he threw out his arms to be picked up, whacking Plugugly eye-wateringly hard on the nose.

'Aaaah,' drooled Plugugly, not minding at all. 'Duz 'oo want a cuddle? Duz 'oo? Den 'oo shall 'ave one. Up 'oo comes. Oooh!' He staggered back, legs buckling as he took Philpot's considerable weight. 'Whoopsie daisy! You *is* gettin' a heavy boy!'

'GA!' said Philpot, playfully biting Plugugly's ear with rock-hard gums. Plugugly didn't mind that either. He jiggled Philpot up and down.

'Is 'oo hungry? Is de bottle empty? Den let's go for our walkies. Is 'oo ready for walkies? *Is* 'oo? *Is* 'oo?'

Philpot kicked him joyfully in the tummy, and he didn't even flinch.

Let's catch up a bit on what has been going on.

It is Plugugly's third day as Nanny Susan, and you will be surprised to hear that things are going brilliantly. Plugugly has found his calling.

The Stonkings have given him his own room, next door to the nursery. It has a proper bed in it! Sleeping in a bed is a revelation. Plugugly lives in a cave with six other Goblins. The sleeping arrangements consist of slumping on top of each other in a pile, like hamsters. Plugugly is usually at the bottom, getting punctured by sharp stones and even sharper Goblin elbows, so having his own bed is luxury indeed.

He gets proper meals too! They arrive three times a day on a tray outside his door. He can even choose what he wants. There are always three courses. Plugugly has decided that he likes pudding best. He has jam pudding for starters, treacle pudding for the main course, and chocolate pudding for pudding. Presumably, the Stonkings employ a cook, although Plugugly never sees her (or him). He never visits the kitchens. He spends all his time up in the nursery with Baby Philpot. He feeds him, winds him, sings to him and plays peek-a-boo with him. He even copes with the nappy side of things, although we won't go into that because this is not a horror story.

Philpot has stopped roaring. He is a very happy baby now. He does nothing but beam at Plugugly, who he loves dearly. Yes, that's right. You heard. Philpot loves Plugugly. Or, rather, he loves Nanny Susan. In particular, Philpot loves the thing that Nanny Susan provides: the *medicine*. He refuses all offers of milk now. Milk is a thing of the past. Philpot currently lives entirely on nettle soup, which he drinks full-time from his huge baby bottle. He can't get enough of it. What's more, he is thriving on it. Instead of roaring, he gurgles. He smiles. He sleeps like an angel. He is a changed character.

You may be wondering how Plugugly is keeping up with the supply and demand. Well, every day, he wraps Philpot up warm, heaves him downstairs (with difficulty, for he is a very *big* baby) and puts him in his pram. Then together, they set off down the long flight of steps to collect the day's supply of nettle soup. This is provided by the rest of the Gaggle, who wait by the gates with a bucket. Plugugly simply refills the giant baby bottle and gives it to Philpot, who grabs it, sucks madly and is once again content.

The Stonkings, of course, are over the moon. They can't do enough for Nanny Susan. They both agree that she is a treasure.

'THERE SHE GOES,' said Bigsy, gazing over the balcony railings. 'NANNY SUSAN. TAKING PHILPOT FOR A WALK.'

'I DON'T KNOW WHAT WE'D DO WITHOUT HER, BIGSY,' said Largette, coming up and slipping an arm around his waist. 'SHE'S A TREASURE. BABY PHILPOT LOVES HER.

WHAT IS HER SECRET?'

'I DUNNO, PETAL. ALL I KNOW IS, HE AIN'T ROARIN'. AT LEAST WE GETS SOME SLEEP NOW.'

'I KNOW,' said Largette, snuggling up to Bigsy. 'I DIDN'T THINK I'D EVER SLEEP AGAIN.'

'HAPPY, PETAL?'

'OH YES, BIGSY. I'M HAPPY THAT BABY PHILPOT'S HAPPY. AND EVEN HAPPIER THAT SOMEONE ELSE IS DEALING WITH HIM. JUST WHILE HE'S GOING THROUGH THE MILK STAGE, OF COURSE.'

'OH YES,' agreed Bigsy. 'WHEN 'E STARTS WALKIN' AN' TALKIN', THAT'S DIFFERENT. WE'LL LIKE 'IM THEN.'

'I KNOW WE WILL. BUT RIGHT NOW, HE'S BETTER OFF WITH A PROFESSIONAL. I WAS THINKING, BIGSY. NOW WE'VE GOT ALL THIS SPARE TIME, WE COULD GO OUT ONE NIGHT, COULDN'T WE? TAKE THE BIKE FOR A SPIN. STOP OFF FOR A BITE TO EAT. PLAY THE JUKEBOX AND DANCE AROUND OUR HELMETS. LIKE WE USED TO DO.'

'YOU MEAN—LEAVE THE BABY?'

'WELL, YES. WE DON'T WANT TO DISTURB HIS ROUTINE. HE'LL BE ALL RIGHT WITH NANNY SUSAN. I DESERVE A BIT OF ME TIME, BIGSY. OH, SAY WE CAN!'

'WHATEVER YOU WANT, PETAL,' said Bigsy fondly. 'WHATEVER YOU WANT.'

*   *   *

Plugugly was down at the gates, where the Gaggle

112

were waiting on the other side of the bars with the bucket.

'You're late,' said Lardo.

'Yes, well, I had to get Baby Philpot ready, didn't I?' said Plugugly.

'Where's the bag o' gold?' demanded Eyesore.

'I hasn't *got* it yet,' said Plugugly. 'I keep *tellin'* you. I gets paid at the end o' the job.'

Hog stood on tiptoe and peered through the bars into the pram, where Philpot lay fretfully waving his empty bottle around.

'Gettin' bigger, innit?' said Hog.

'Is you referrin' to Baby Philpot?' asked Plugugly coldly. 'Because he isn't an it.'

'Yeah, whatever. I'm just sayin' it's grown. Don't you fink, Stinkwart?'

'I dunno,' said Stinkwart with a surly shrug. 'Dunno 'ow big it's s'posed to be. Don't care, neither.'

'Did Stinkwart speak?' Plugugly enquired of the other Goblins. 'Did I 'ear 'im say sumfink? I must say I'm surprised he's here. I'm surprised he isn't out *stick-collectin'*.' He leant into the pram and fussed about with Philpot's blanket. 'Take no notice o' dat bad Goblin, Baby Philpot. He don't know nuffin'.'

Stinkwart scowled and wandered off to kick a bush.

'Hold out his bottle, then,' said Lardo, picking up the rusty bucket. 'I'll fill it up.'

Plugugly removed the teat and stuck the bottle through the bars. Lardo tipped up the bucket and attempted to pour in the contents. They came out in a rush. Most ended up coating Plugugly's hand. The rest formed a puddle on the ground.

'Look at dat!' said Plugugly crossly, wiping his gunky hand on his apron. 'You is one careless Goblin, Lardo.'

'You shoulda kept the bottle still,' said Lardo. ''Ow am I s'posed to pour if you keep wavin' it around?'

'But dere's hardly any in dere! What's Baby Philpot gonna do?'

'Ah, stop fussin'. We'll scrape it up off the ground.'

'But den it's all dirty!'

'So? He's eating nettles, crushed berries, mud an' rust. What's dirt gonna do?'

This was true.

'Well, hurry up,' said Plugugly. 'If he don't get fed, he gets sad.'

In the pram, Philpot was indeed getting restless. His brow was creased and his clenched fists waved around. His bulging eyes were fixed on the bottle. If he didn't get it soon, there was going to be trouble.

The Gaggle—well, all except Stinkwart, who was still away bush-kicking—set about the task of scooping up the spilled nettle soup with dirty cupped hands and transferring it into the bottle. A lot of it had soaked into the ground. Despite their best efforts, the bottle was only half full. And that included quite a lot of grass, leaves and twigs. It was a lot thicker than usual.

'GA!' bellowed Philpot from the pram, making everyone jump. 'GA! GAGAGAGAG . . .'

Hastily, Plugugly thrust the half-full bottle into Philpot's hands. He stuck it into his mouth and commenced sucking noisily.

'You see?' said Lardo. 'He likes it with extra

114

dirt.'

He was right. Philpot did.

CHAPTER FOURTEEN

PREPARATIONS

In Witchway Wood, all talk was about the forth-coming O'Lumpick Games. You couldn't avoid the subject. For a start, every other tree sported one of Vincent's posters. Black background with dribbly blood red writing.

THE O'LUMPICKS ARE COMING! they screamed. *OPEN TO ALL!*

The Daily Miracle was full of it and the spellovision news talked of nothing else. Not that anybody read the paper or watched spellovision much. They were all too busy doing knee bends and eating cauliflower. Besides, you could have enough of Sourmuddle, who was never off the screen, claiming that the O'Lumpick Games were all her idea.

There was a new spirit in the Wood. Suddenly, everyone took to wearing shorts. There was talk of *getting fit* and *eating healthily*. If you took a stroll before breakfast, most likely you would come across the Skeleton team jogging, or the Troll team doing press-ups. Sometimes you might see the Mummies, Xotindis and Xstufitu, sharing a delicious banana before resuming their speed walk. If you were really lucky you might see the faddy Werewolf from the sweet shop queue sprint past, slip on the skin and fall over.

Everyone was taking the preparations seriously. The Banshees hired Witchway Hall every Monday night for a step aerobics class. On Tuesdays, the Zombies took it over for weightlifting practice. There were earnest discussions about what to wear for the Opening Parade, and what should go on the flag. The Witchway Rhythm Boys began practising marching music.

Nobody was keener than the Witches. Pongwiffy's rousing speech had pricked their consciences and made them take a long, hard look at themselves. All of them had gone back to their caves and cottages, rifled through their cupboards and thrown out all the bad stuff. Then they all went on a strict exercise regime. Sludgegooey took up jogging. Bendyshanks went in for Yoga. Gaga found an old bicycle and could be seen screeching around at all hours of the day and night. Ratsnappy, Scrofula and Greymatter met up twice a day to do stretching exercises. Macabre practised tossing large tree trunks around. (Everyone kept a wide berth.) The twins started skipping. Even Bonidle could be seen late at night, sleep running. Sharkadder started up a Keep Fit class on Wednesday nights, which was proving popular. And Pongwiffy herself ran around like a mad thing, organising.

Much to the Yetis' dismay, business at *Sugary*

Candy's was beginning to drop off. The daily queues dwindled. Nobody wanted sweets any more. Sweets were out, sprouts were in. The Yetis finally put a sign on the door. It said: CLOSED UNTIL FURTHER NOTICE. Then they turned off the lights, fastened the magic padlock and went off to have emergency business meetings behind locked doors.

The Sports Committee were holding one of their regular meetings at Sharkadder's. They were gathered around her table, on which was set a healthy bowl of pickled cucumbers and a pile of entry forms.

'It's proving even more popular than I thought,' said Pongwiffy. 'Just look at all those forms. Everyone wants to take part. How many teams are entering?'

'Twelve,' said Greymatter, looking at her notepad. 'There's us, the Familiars, the Skeletons, the Trolls, the Zombies, the Banshees, the Mummies, the Vampires, the Ghosts, the Ghouls and the Gnomes. And that dithering Werewolf. He's in a team on his own. He's entering for the Relay, I'm not sure how.'

'My word,' marvelled Pongwiffy. 'Twelve teams! And they'll all have supporters. I bet crowds will come from far and wide.'

'Ah don't know how crowds from far an' wide'll fit in Futtout's garden,' said Macabre. 'It's big, but it's no that big.'

'It'll be a squeeze,' admitted Pongwiffy, 'but there has to be an audience, doesn't there, Hugo? To cheer and clap and stuff. Right, moving on. Have you thought about the Parade costumes, Sharky?'

119

'I have,' said Sharkadder coyly. 'But they're a secret. I don't want anyone to see them yet. They're rather marvellous, though. I'm thinking dazzling, vibrant colours.'

'Hmm,' said Pongwiffy, mentally resolving that whatever Sharkadder came up with, she would hide it under her old cardigan. 'What's next on the list, Greymatter?'

'Prepare the stadium,' read out Greymatter. 'Chop trees, pull up roses, remove statues, mark out running track with whitewash. Build podium. Bring over the chairs from Witchway Hall. And put up the bunting.'

'Where is the bunting?' Pongwiffy wanted to know. The bunting consisted of lots of rather faded little coloured flags strung out on a length of heavily knotted string. It always got dragged out on festive occasions.

'Under the hall platform, I think.'

'Well, somebody find it. I can't waste time hunting for bunting. I'll get cracking on the stadium straight away. I'll take a team of Familiars along first thing tomorrow.'

Hugo, Rory, Dudley and Speks rolled their eyes at each other and sighed.

'And you can stop all that!' scolded Pongwiffy. 'Just because you're in a team doesn't mean you get let off work. Any further business, Greymatter?'

'I think that's it, for now. Oh, almost forgot. There's a special Coven Meeting tonight. Sourmuddle's asking for a report on how it's all going. And we've got to decide how we're going to organise the Witch team.'

'Do the Familiars have to come?' enquired Rory.

'No,' said Greymatter. 'You're our rivals now. We don't want you listening in. Spying and stealing our ideas.'

'As if,' said Hugo.

'Don't flatter yerselves,' scoffed Rory.

'I don't *think* so,' growled Dudley.

'We've got our own ideas,' sniffed Speks. 'We don't need to copy yours.'

'Well, that remains to be seen, doesn't it?' said Greymatter. 'Anyway, it's a Witches only meeting and you're not allowed to come.'

'Right,' said Pongwiffy. 'I think we've covered everything. My, I'm stiff with all that sitting. Time for a spot of exercise. You Familiars are dismissed. Everybody else on your feet. Deep breaths, follow me. Running on the spot, then three times around the table. Hup, two, three, four, hup, two, three, four . . .'

*   *   *

The rest of the Familiars were gathered together in an old barn on the edge of the Wood, waiting for Hugo, Dudley, Speks and Rory to arrive. Just so that you are clear who they all are, let's run through them. The Familiars are:

Vernon, Ratsnappy's Rat. Currently eating a cheese sandwich on an upturned bucket.

Filth, Sludgegooey's Fiend, perched on a barrel, air drumming with his eyes closed. He has just finished rehearsal.

IdentiKit and CopiCat, Agglebag and Bagaggle's Siamese Cats, elegantly arranged on a bale of straw and looking bored.

Gaga's Bats, hanging upside down from a rafter.

122

Slithering Steve, Bendyshanks' Grass Snake, curled up on top of a flowerpot.

Bonidle's nameless Sloth, snoozing in a pile of hay.

Scrofula's Vulture, Barry, hunched in a corner, not feeling too well.

Snoop, Sourmuddle's Demon, is not present. Like his mistress, he has expressed disinterest in Sport. He considers himself too grand for it, particularly if it involves wearing shorts. (Tail difficulties.) He is currently back home doing the crossword in *The Demon Times*, watching his mistress being interviewed on spellovision.

Sourmuddle, whilst not prepared to actively participate in the O'Lumpicks, is certainly not averse to talking about them. She can be seen pretty well every night, appearing on spellovision talk shows, taking all the credit. She regularly announces that she has every confidence that the Witch team will win every event and take home all the gold medals. This is fighting talk, guaranteed to annoy everyone and make every team determined to prove her wrong, particularly the Familiars.

The Familiars don't often get together. They only meet up at the monthly Coven Meeting. Their Witches keep them very busy, and besides, they don't get on amongst themselves. There is a lot of inter-species rivalry and petty bickering. But they are entering the O'Lumpicks as a team, so for now it is important to set aside their differences. There's the flag to think about for a start. Everybody has strong views on this.

'It's got to be big,' said Vernon. 'It's got to be seen in the back row. I see a big white banner with

THE FABULOUS FAMILIARS written on it in huge black letters.'

'Oh *purleeeze!*' drawled IdentiKit. 'Black on white, that's what *everyone* will do.'

'Far too obvious,' agreed CopiCat. 'Typical of a Rat to come up with something common like that.'

'Trust you two to be negative,' snapped Vernon. 'Suggest something else, then.'

'I always think green is a very nice colour,' piped up Slithering Steve shyly.

'Yes, well, you're green so you would say that,' said Vernon. 'We should keep it simple and use a white sheet.'

'Aw, man,' said Filth. 'What's with the sheet thing, dude? Where's the bling in that, bro?'

'I'm just saying,' snapped Vernon crossly. 'I'm just saying that using a white sheet is the obvious way to go. We can't spend hours making a flag. Not when we're supposed to be getting into training, not to mention all the other things we have to do . . .'

Just then, the barn door crashed open and in came Rory, Hugo, Speks and Dudley, hotfoot from the meeting of the Sports Committee. The barn was situated quite a long way from Sharkadder's and they had run all the way, for exercise.

'Phew!' panted Rory. 'Ah'm puffed oot! Ah think ma hooves are on fire.' He blew on his feet, which were indeed smoking.

'How did the meeting go?' enquired Barry. 'Did you learn anything new?'

'Zey vant us to start preparing stadium,' Hugo told him. 'All Familiars got to meet in ze palace garden tomorrow. Start choppink ze trees down.'

'Not me,' said Filth. 'Band rehearsal, man.'

124

'You see?' cried Vernon. 'There's no time to fiddle around with complicated colour schemes. Keep it simple, I say.'

'Keep what simple?' growled Dudley.

'We're talking about our flag,' explained Steve. 'Vernon wants it to be white with black letters.'

'Which is like, dull, man!' cried Filth. 'Ain't no one gonna respect a banner like that.'

'I must say I agree with Filth,' said Speks. 'The Witches are wearing vibrant costumes. We don't want them outshining us. We're a team to be reckoned with. We want everyone to sit up and take notice when we enter the arena. Perhaps there should be some kind of logo.'

'*Oi* knows what'd make 'em take notice,' growled Dudley. 'A skull an' crossbones, that'd show 'em we mean business.'

'Is Sports Day, not pirate convention,' sneered Hugo. 'Zat rubbish idea.'

'You gotta better one, furball?'

'You talkink to me?'

'Yeah. Wanna make somethin' of it?'

'Yeah!'

'Yeah?'

'Oh yeah!'

We will leave them here. A fight breaks out, and it's not pretty. But you will be relieved to hear that they suddenly remember that it's all about Sport and teamwork and eventually get back to discussing the flag.

CHAPTER FIFTEEN

SOLIDS

Plugugly sat in the nursery with Philpot on his lap. On the floor next to him was a large, empty pudding basin with a spoon in it.

'De wheels on de boat go in an' up, off an' down, on an' out,' sang Plugugly. He didn't know many nursery songs and usually got the words wrong, but Philpot didn't seem to care. 'De wheels on de boat go in an' up, dum-dee-long.'

'GA!' gurgled Philpot sleepily. 'GA!'

'You want it again? Den you shall. De wheels on de boat go . . .'

There came a timid little knock on the door. Hastily, Plugugly kicked the pudding basin under the crib.

'Yes?' trilled Plugugly. 'Who dat?'

'ONLY ME, NANNY SUSAN,' came Largette's voice. 'CAN I COME IN?'

'Yes,' called Plugugly. 'But you has got to be

quiet. I is gettin' Baby Philpot off to sleep.'

The door opened and Largette peeped in. She was wearing a pink leather jacket and matching leather trousers. Under her arm was a pink helmet.

'AHHH,' she breathed. 'MY BABY! HIS EYES ARE NEARLY CLOSED.'

'Yes,' said Plugugly. 'Dat's 'cos he is nearly asleep.'

'I DON'T KNOW HOW YOU DO IT, NANNY SUSAN. YOU HAVE SUCH A WAY WITH HIM.'

Plugugly glowed. It was true. He did have a way with Philpot.

'DID HE DRINK UP ALL HIS MILK TODAY?' enquired Largette, the concerned mother.

'Um—yes,' lied Plugugly.

'THAT'S WONDERFUL. NOT LONG BEFORE WE SEE A LITTLE TOOTH POKING THROUGH. THEN HE CAN GO ON TO SOLIDS.'

'Yes.'

'HE'LL REALLY BEGIN SHOOTING UP THEN. ALTHOUGH HE'S GROWING QUITE FAST NOW, ISN'T HE?'

'Mmm,' said Plugugly.

'IS IT NORMAL, DO YOU THINK? HOW FAST HE'S GROWING?'

'Oh yes,' said Plugugly.

'IT'S JUST THAT HE SEEMS A LOT BIGGER THAN OTHER BABIES HIS AGE. CAN HE STILL FIT IN HIS PRAM?'

'Yes,' said Plugugly. 'Just about.'

'IT'S JUST THAT THE OTHER DAY I

NOTICED YOU—WELL, *JAMMING* HIM IN. SORT OF *RAMMING* HIM DOWN. HIS FEET STICK OUT AT THE END, DON'T THEY?'

'Mmm.'

'WELL, HE CERTAINLY SEEMS HAPPY,' said Largette. 'YOU'RE DOING A WONDERFUL JOB.'

'Yes.'

'I JUST POPPED IN TO SAY BIGSY AND ME ARE POPPING OUT FOR A LITTLE SPIN ON THE BIKE. IF THAT'S ALL RIGHT WITH YOU.'

'Dat's all right.'

'I'LL LEAVE YOU TO IT, THEN.' Respectfully, Largette tiptoed out.

Philpot was properly asleep now. Plugugly stood up, staggered across and heaved him into his crib, which sagged under the weight. It really was getting much too small. Philpot spilled over the sides. Even with his head rammed hard against the top end, his feet stuck out a mile.

This is all wrong, of course. Philpot should be growing a bit, but not this much. He is only one week old. By rights, there are another two weeks to go before he cuts his first tooth and starts shooting up. But Philpot is different. Instead of milk, he has been living on nettle soup, which has had the effect of vastly accelerating his growth rate.

Actually, soup is no longer the right word. Soup implies something liquid, something sloshy. But over the last few days, the Goblins have been experimenting with the pretend medicine formula. They have been adding all kinds of stuff to the bucket. Grass, twigs, gravel, leaves, quicksand,

129

toadstools, anything they can find. The resultant mess is now so thick that it is more like cake than medicine. Plugugly has abandoned the bottle and feeds it to Philpot out of a bowl, with a spoon.

So. Philpot is now on solids. And boy, does he love them.

If you put a finger in Philpot's mouth and felt his gums—inadvisable, by the way—you wouldn't find just one tooth. You would find loads! All his teeth are coming through at the same time, much too early. Amazingly, this isn't hurting him at all. Philpot loves the fact that his teeth are coming through because he can use them to masticate his medicine.

Love is blind. Plugugly is vaguely aware that Philpot is getting very big, but he pushes any anxious thoughts to one side. After all, Philpot is happy now and Plugugly likes to see him happy. What harm can it do, spoiling him a bit?

Philpot lay crammed into his crib, sucking his thumb, deep in the world of nod.

'Rock-a-bye Philpot, in de tea pot,' crooned Plugugly tunelessly. The rockers creaked alarmingly under Philpot's weight. 'When you wakes up, I'll give you yer pretend medicine; when yer pretend medicine's gone we'll la lala la . . .'

'MEDSIN!' muttered Philpot happily.

It was his first proper word.

$$* \qquad * \qquad *$$

The rest of the Gaggle were restless. The days were going by, and there was still no sign of any gold. They were getting bored of traipsing to and fro with buckets of baby food too. Instead of the whole Gaggle going, they were now taking it in turns.

Today, it was Eyesore's turn. He came marching back into the cave and threw the empty bucket into a corner.

'Still no bag o' gold, then,' said Hog.

'No,' said Eyesore shortly. ''E just filled the bowl an' went. I asked 'im, but 'e said 'e'd gimme a black eye if I mentioned it again.'

'I'm sure it's bin a week,' said Lardo. ''Ow many days in a week?'

Nobody knew. Sproggit suggested ten, but he was only guessing.

'Well, all I know is, it's been a long time,' went on Hog. ''Ow much longer we gotta wait? I wants to go shoppin' fer sweeties *now*.'

The Goblins had been talking a lot about shopping for sweets. They had long, argumentative discussions about *Sugary Candy's* and what it would be like. Plugugly's description of its glories had whetted their appetites and given their brains something to chew on. They desperately wanted to go and see it for themselves, but didn't dare because there was a lot of activity in Witchway Wood at the moment. The Witches in particular seemed to be doing a lot of running around, and as we know, Witches and Goblins don't get on. So the Gaggle had to restrict themselves to imagining. Goblins have limited imaginations, so the conversations tended to be samey.

'Sweeties,' said Sproggit dreamily. 'Rows an' rows o' great big jars, Plug said. Imagine.'

'I hope there's red ones,' said Lardo, drooling. 'I loves red ones.'

'An' green ones,' said Slopbucket. 'An' yeller

131

ones. An' blue ones. An' orange ones. An' pink ones an' purple ones an' brown ones an' grey ones an' . . .'

'That's enough colours,' said Stinkwart, adding, 'An' you don't get grey sweets.'

'How do you know? You gets all kinda colours.' Slopbucket went off into his drone again. 'Grey ones an' green ones an' yeller ones an' blue ones an' orange ones an' pink ones an' purple ones an' brown ones an' pink ones an . . .'

'You said pink twice,' pointed out Hog.

'Ah, but that's 'cos there's two jars of 'em.'

'You don't know that,' argued Stinkwart.

'Niver do you, so shut up,' said Slopbucket.

There was a little pause.

'Someone should go an' fill the medicine bucket for tomorrer,' said Eyesore.

'Yeah,' said Hog. 'Someone should.'

Nobody stirred.

CHAPTER SIXTEEN

GETTING CLOSER

Nobody was late to the full Coven Meeting. All thirteen chairs were occupied. There were no sweets to be seen either. Instead, everyone had brought along neat little plastic containers packed with celery, carrot sticks and apples. Even better, no one was complaining of aches and pains. Sallow faces and tooth problems belonged in the past. Everyone looked fitter and sat straighter. Clearly, the new regime was beginning to work.

'Right!' shouted Sourmuddle, rapping her Wand on the table. 'Attention, everyone. First, I want an update from the Sports Committee. Make it quick, though, I'm on the *Ali Pali Show* in half an hour. Speak up, Pongwiffy. Is everything on track?'

'Absolutely!' cried Pongwiffy. 'All the entry forms are in and I'm taking a team of Familiars along to sort out the stadium.'

'What's happening about our flag?' chipped in Bendyshanks.

'Ah'm workin' on it,' said Macabre. 'Ah'm thinking big banner. Moon, stars, an' thirteen Witches flying across on Broomsticks. *The Winning Witches* written on it in big letters.'

'Sounds good, we'll leave it to you,' said Pongwiffy. 'So now it's all down to talking athletics. We have to decide who does what.'

There was a hum of excitement. This was the moment they had all been waiting for.

'Pass me the list,' ordered Sourmuddle. 'I'm Grandwitch, I decide. Right. Who wants to do the Three-Legged Race?'

'Me and Ag!' shouted Bagaggle, before anyone could open their mouths. 'We've been practising, haven't we?'

'We have, Bag,' agreed Agglebag.

Indeed they had. They had taken to doing everything with their ankles roped together. They even slept like it. Difficult in the mornings, when they forgot and got up on opposite sides of the bed.

'Fair enough,' said Sourmuddle. 'Moving on. Egg and Spoon.'

'*Me!*' came a number of voices. Pongwiffy was loudest of all. She fancied her chances at the Egg and Spoon.

'Sludgegooey,' said Sourmuddle decisively. 'You're covered in egg stains anyway, so it won't matter if you fall over when you're practising. You'd better not drop it on the day, though.'

'I won't,' said Sludgegooey smugly. 'I'll win for the Witches, you'll see.'

'You'd better. Right. Weightlifting.'

'Um—' began Pongwiffy, too late again.

'*Me!*' shouted Ratsnappy. 'It's got to be me,

134

Sourmuddle. I've been doing press-ups with Vernon. I'm getting these huge muscles in my arms, see? Look how they're stretching my cardigan.'

'All right. Ratsnappy's our weightlifter. Next, High Jump.'

'Er—' said Pongwiffy, but was overshadowed. Gaga had leapt from her chair and was bouncing around, wild with excitement.

'Yes, all right, Gaga, you can do it, calm down,' said Sourmuddle, and Gaga leapt twice over the table before collapsing in a corner, overcome with happiness.

'Who wants to do the Sack Race?' went on Sourmuddle.

'I do,' attempted Pongwiffy, but was silenced by Sharkadder's sharp elbow in her ribs.

'*I* rather fancy that,' said Sharkadder.

'Fine. Tossing the Caber next. I take it that'll be you, Macabre?'

'It will,' said Macabre, adding threateningly, 'or Ah'll want tay know the reason why.'

'Hey, listen—' cut in Pongwiffy again, but no one was listening.

'That leaves four for the Relay,' said Sourmuddle. 'Greymatter, Bonidle, Bendyshanks and Scrofula. That's it, all decided.'

'Wait a minute!' shouted Pongwiffy. 'What am *I* doing? You've missed me out.'

'Have I? Oh well. Tough.'

'But that's not *fair*! The O'Lumpicks were my idea and I'm doing most of the organising and now you're saying I can't compete?'

'So? *I'm* not competing, am I?'

'But you don't *want* to!' cried Pongwiffy crossly.

135

'All you want to do is go on spello and take all the credit.'

'Yes? So?'

'So I want to be in them! I should be in them, shouldn't I?'

Pongwiffy appealed to the assembled company, who shrugged and looked away. What did they care if Pongwiffy wasn't in them? They were.

'Sharky?' she said piteously. 'Don't *you* have anything to say?' Surely her best friend would be on her side?

'Yes,' said Sharkadder. 'Get over it. I'm sorry, Pong, but you said yourself that Sourmuddle's decision is final. Now, I've brought my tape measure with me and I need to take everyone's measurements for the costumes. So if you'd all line up . . .'

'Stay right where you are!' bellowed Pongwiffy. 'I've been doing all the healthy eating and exercising and stuff. If I don't get to be in them, I'm going on strike and there won't *be* an O'Lumpicks, so there. Unless someone else wants to do all the donkey work. Any volunteers?'

Nobody put a hand up. Sourmuddle went into a huddle with Snoop.

'You see?' said Pongwiffy. 'I didn't think so.'

'All right,' said Sourmuddle suddenly. 'You can be in them.'

'I can? Doing what?'

'You can lead the Grand Opening Parade. You can have the honour of holding the flag. That's an important job, isn't it?'

Pongwiffy thought about this. Actually, it was. Participating in the Games would have been good, of course—but to be there up front, the first one

136

in, holding the flag and leading the Parade—well, that was special. She could imagine the cheers.

'Really?' she said.

'Really. You're the official Flag Holder.'

'You won't change your mind at the last moment?'

'You have my word.'

'All right,' said Pongwiffy. 'In that case—all right.'

'Good old Pong,' sang Sharkadder. 'My Flag Holding Friend. I'll make sure your costume is the most vibrant of all.'

'Mmm,' said Pongwiffy. She cheered up, though, and even allowed herself to be measured.

*   *   *

'The paper hasn't arrived again, Futtout,' said Queen Beryl. 'I haven't seen it for days. I haven't a clue what's going on in the Wood.'

'Really, dearest? Deary me.'

It was the following morning, and once again the royal family were gathered at the breakfast table. King Futtout was having a soft boiled egg, Queen Beryl had strong coffee and dry toast and Honeydimple had jam doughnuts with hot fudge sauce and pink sprinkles.

'Write and complain, Futtout. Insist that they sack the paper boy.'

'I will,' promised King Futtout. He wouldn't, of course. He had cancelled the paper. He didn't want Queen Beryl to read the headlines, oh dear me no.

'Futtout!' rapped Queen Beryl suddenly. She had gone very stiff and her eyes were trained on the garden. 'What is *this* I see through the window?'

King Futtout's watery gaze followed her pointing finger. He gave a little start.

'Oh,' he said. 'Erm—oh.'

Slap bang in the middle of the lawn, under a spreading chestnut tree, was an unmistakable figure. Pongwiffy with a clipboard, surrounded by her working party of Familiars, all armed to the teeth with a number of businesslike tools.

'What is *she* doing here?' demanded Queen Beryl. 'And why has she brought that raggle-taggle band of—*creatures*? That great hairy *thing* with the horns! And all those evil-looking cats! And that hideous bald vulture!'

'Erm—pets, possibly?'

'Thum petth,' said Honeydimple, through a mouthful of doughnut. 'Don't be thilly, Daddy.'

'They've got axes, Futtout! Axes and buckets of whitewash! And spades, and ladders! And a great long piece of string with tacky little *flags* on! *Why*, Futtout?'

'I really have no idea, dearest,' squeaked King Futtout, bashing weakly at his egg.

'Surely they can't be going ahead with that appalling O'Lumpick idea! It's an outrage! After sending that letter.'

'Mmm.' Bash, bash, bash.

'You did *send* the letter, Futtout?'

'Erm. Yes.' King Futtout gave a little cough. 'Yes, most definitely.'

'No you didn't, Daddy,' said Honeydimple. 'You hid it under the cushion, I *thaw* you.'

'Futtout!' thundered Queen Beryl. 'Go out there now and tell her to go away. And take those dreadful creatures with her. There's a *snake*. Uggh!'

'But I still haven't—'

'*Now.*'

'But my egg—'

'*Do it!*'

Trembling, King Futtout abandoned breakfast and went off to do it.

Over on the lawn, Pongwiffy was issuing instructions. All the Familiars were present and correct apart from Snoop (back home keeping the Broom company), Filth (band rehearsal) and Bonidle's Sloth (excused on account of sleep. When it came to practical activities, it was more trouble than it was worth).

'Right,' said Pongwiffy. 'Steve, you're in charge of marking out the running tracks. Just dive in the bucket of whitewash and crawl along. *Straight*, mind. Try not to wriggle too much.'

'How many lines?' asked Steve.

'I don't know, do I? Lots. Keep going until you run out of lawn. You Bats, you can start hanging up the bunting. Barry can help with that.'

'I'd rather not,' said Barry. 'Bit of a headache, overdid the exercise. I'd sooner not fly.'

'Then make a start digging up those rose bushes, they're in the way. You Cats can help. Don't look like that, CopiCat and IdentiKit, we're all pulling our weight. Rory and Vernon, you can start dismantling the gazebo—oh. Here's Futtout, come to help. Dudley, give him an axe.'

Poor King Futtout came trailing up, looking terrified.

'Erm—my wife,' he mumbled. Dudley tried to hand him an axe, and he backed away.

'What about her?'

'My wife is not too—erm—pleased. Not too—you know—keen.'

'About what?'

'About the whole idea, really. This—erm—O'Lumpicks business.'

'Well, she should be keen. Very keen indeed. Everybody else is. Haven't you been watching spellovision?'

'No,' confessed King Futtout. They didn't have a spellovision set in the palace. The King would have liked one, but was overruled by Queen Beryl on the grounds that people might enjoy it.

'Well, it's wall-to-wall O'Lumpick coverage. The whole Wood's O'Lumpick crazy. The whole *world's* O'Lumpick crazy! Do you want it going out on the news that you've refused permission to use your grounds? At this late stage? There'll be riots.'

King Futtout bit his lip. Which was he more scared of? Millions of rioting sports enthusiasts or Queen Beryl?

'*What* is going on here?' The sharp voice rang out from behind them. Queen Beryl came marching across the lawn, almost tripping over Steve, who had obediently coated himself in whitewash and was carefully wriggling out his first line. 'I demand an explanation!'

'Ask him,' said Pongwiffy cheerfully, pointing at King Futtout. '*He* knows. Oi! You Bats! Mind out with that bunting, you're getting it all tangled! Not in *that* tree, you idiots, *that* tree's coming down! I dunno, Bats, Vultures, who'd work with 'em, eh?'

'Futtout! Are you just going to stand there, or are you going to *do* something?' demanded Queen Beryl.

140

'She's right, you know,' agreed Pongwiffy. 'No room for slackers. Go and get your shed cleared out, Futtout. My friend needs it to store the costumes. Get Beryl here to help, she looks like she could do with the exercise. I can't stay chatting. Got things to do, places to go, people to see. Hugo, stay here and take over. I'm off to visit Scott. I'm calling for Sharky, she's coming with me. She says she needs a break from the sewing machine. By Scott I am referring to Scott Sinister, the famous film star, you know, a personal friend of mine. A *proper* celebrity.' She gave Queen Beryl a withering glare. '*He* does what he's told.'

And off she went, leaving the royal couple to row amongst themselves. Well, Queen Beryl rowed. King Futtout just stood there and hung his head. I suppose we should feel sorry for him, but he is so very wet.

*   *   *

On the other side of Witchway Wood, Scott Sinister sat in his study, tongue out, madly scribbling on a piece of paper with a quill pen.

Once again he had been bullied into cooperating with Witches, which in the past had been disastrous. But maybe, this time, everything might turn out all right. After all, the O'Lumpicks were different. It was Sport. Everyone was supposed to play fair and be good losers if they didn't win. It wasn't all bad.

And of course, Pongwiffy was right. Think of the publicity! Scott was a professional. His many fans would be watching, both in the flesh and on spello-vision, desperate for a glimpse of their hero. They would be hanging on his every word.

Scott was determined to do a good job. In fact, in a flash of inspiration, he had come up with a rather novel idea. Introducing the various competing teams *in poetry*, no less. Nobody had told him which teams were actually competing, but he thought he'd have a bash anyway and see how he got on.

'Wizards,' muttered Scott. 'Bizzards, cizzards, dizzards, fizzards, gizzards. Lizards. Blizzards. Hmm.'

'What are you doing, Scott?' said a voice in his ear. Scott jumped a mile, knocking over the ink-pot. A black tide spread across the desk and dripped into his lap.

Standing behind him were two Witches, Broomsticks in hand. Pongwiffy and Sharkadder, both smiling at him, a bit out of breath from the flight. Pongwiffy was her usual dishevelled self. Sharkadder was a vision in purple, with matching lipstick.

'Don't *do* that,' he snapped, dabbing himself with a hanky. 'Who let you in? Look what you've made me do!'

'We let ourselves in,' explained Pongwiffy. 'Flew straight in through the downstairs window. Can't be bothered with butlers. You remember my friend, Witch Sharkadder?'

'Yes,' said Scott shortly. 'I do.' His tone was rather bitter. There had been a certain incident in the past involving Sharkadder, himself and a beauty demonstration that went horribly wrong. Well, let's put it like this. He lost a lot of face.

'Hello, Mr Sinister,' trilled Sharkadder. 'Lovely to see you again. I expect you're all excited? With it being the Big Day next Saturday?'

'Leave it to me to do the talking, Sharky, if you please,' said Pongwiffy firmly. 'He's my friend.'

'Did you say *next Saturday*?'

'Time flies, doesn't it, Scott?' agreed Pongwiffy. 'I hope you're prepared. It's a very important job, commentating. Nobody'll know what's happening unless someone's explaining it.'

'*I* don't know what's happening.' Scott pointed out rather crossly. 'I'd appreciate a little direction. I don't even know what the games are, or who's in them or *anything*.'

'Yes, well, it's all a bit complicated, organising a whole O'Lumpicks,' said Pongwiffy. 'We're still working things out. But it'll all come together in the end. If it's any help, the first thing you have to do is introduce the teams in the Grand Opening Parade.'

'Well, yes. I've been thinking about that,' said Scott. 'In fact, I've had a rather good idea. I'm thinking of welcoming each team with a short rhyming couplet. I have a couple here, if you'd like to . . . ?'

'Go ahead,' said Pongwiffy. 'Although I don't know what poetry's got to do with Sport.'

'*Clap your hands and shout and scream,*
Here comes the amazingly fit and wonderful Skeleton team.'

'Not bad,' said Pongwiffy. 'Although I'd shorten it a bit. Cut out *amazingly fit and wonderful* and I think you're there.'

'I've got another one,' said Scott.

'You have?'

'*They come from the mountain, where there's blizzards.*

143

Welcome to the gallant, athletic Wizards.'

'They're not athletic,' scoffed Pongwiffy. '*Pathetic*, more like. Anyway, they haven't sent in an entry form, so you've wasted your time there. Have you done one for us Witches?'

'Not yet.'

'Well, make sure it's good. Make it longer than the others. We're far and away the best team, so we want the rhymiest introduction. Use words like *astonishingly fit and toned.'*

'And *vibrantly costumed,'* added Sharkadder.

'Yes,' said Pongwiffy. 'If you must. Although I don't think it'll be easy finding a rhyme.'

'But he'll try,' said Sharkadder. 'Won't you, Scott?'

'And he'll pop in a line about the Flag Holder, I expect?' added Pongwiffy.

Both of them beamed at him.

'Yes' said Scott wearily. 'I'll try.'

CHAPTER SEVENTEEN

A MEETING WITH RONALD

You may remember that the Wizards had refused to enter for the O'Lumpicks. Well, all but one. Ronald the Magnificent, Sharkadder's nephew, who we last saw being roundly jeered at for showing interest in them. It didn't put him off, though.

Ronald was really excited at the whole idea of the forthcoming Games. Of course, he didn't say so. But he couldn't stop thinking about them.

Every day, he waited impatiently until everyone had finished with *The Daily Miracle* and hurled it disdainfully into the bin. He would sneakily fish it out with trembling fingers and run upstairs to his room to pore over the latest thrilling O'Lumpick news.

The pages were full of pictures of the various competing teams, grinning at the camera with their thumbs up. Everyone wore shorts and clutched little bottles of water. There were interviews with Skeletons, Trolls, Ghouls, Banshees and Zombies, each claiming to have developed a unique, foolproof training programme. Instead of advertisements for *Sugary Candy's*, there were full page spreads dedicated to healthy eating. Sharkadder's Lemon Sprouts were proving particularly popular. Getting fit was the order of the day. There were a lot of gossip columns debating what costumes the athletes might wear in the Grand Opening Parade. Everyone was being very secretive, particularly about the design of their flag.

Sometimes, when the rest of the Wizards were snoozing in the lounge, Ronald tried turning on the spellovision, hoping to catch a glimpse of what was going on. He kept the volume low, but even so, someone always woke up and ordered him to turn it off, just to be mean. But the glimpses only whetted his appetite.

Just imagine it! A whole day devoted to Sport! Out in the fresh air! Wearing shorts!

Ronald had a pair of shorts. They were baggy and yellow. He had only worn them once, on a trip to the seaside. He kept them in his bottom drawer.

He pictured himself wearing them again. Strolling around casually chatting to his fellow competitors. Everyone saying, 'Who is that young Wizard in the yellow shorts? He looks like a strong contender.'

What a change that would make from eating sausages and sitting around in the overheated lounge talking vaguely about Magic but hardly ever doing any. Ronald got bored sometimes. The only time he went out was to do the weekly sweet run. Being the youngest Wizard, he either got ignored or picked on, with nothing in between. It didn't help that his aunt was a Witch either. He got a lot of stick for that.

Imagine if he competed in the O'Lumpicks, though! Competed, and won a gold medal! Things would be different then. The Wizards would have to clap him on the back and sing *For He's A Jolly Good Wizard*. Maybe carry him back to the Clubhouse shoulder-high. Frame the medal and hang it in the foyer. Show him a bit of respect, for once.

Ronald sent off for an entry form. When it arrived, he scuttled down at the crack of dawn, snatched it from the doorstep, then hurried up to his room to study it in secret.

He skipped over the first bit, which looked boring, and went straight to the list of games, looking for ones he thought he would be good at.

The Three-Legged Race was out because there was only one of him. The Sack Race was out because it needed practice with a sack. He could try begging one from the kitchens, but didn't hold out much hope because the cook didn't like him. Tossing the Caber was out. He didn't know what a caber was, or why it needed tossing. The elastic on his shorts was a bit feeble, so the High Jump presented major risks. Weightlifting sounded like hard work, and he would be up against Trolls and Zombies and probably Pongwiffy's Hamster, who was a lot stronger than he looked. The Relay was a non-starter, as there was no one to pass the baton to. That left one race. The Egg and Spoon. The Wizards specialised in breakfast, so getting hold of the props to practise with was easy.

Ronald filled in the entry form. Where it said TEAM NAME, he wrote *Ronald the Magnificent* in his best handwriting. He wrote it again in the space opposite Egg and Spoon. Then he sent it off, with a second-class stamp because he'd run out of first-class and didn't dare ask to borrow one in case he got quizzed about why he wanted it.

Every morning, when his fellow Wizards staggered from the dining room to the lounge, Ronald secreted away a boiled egg and silver spoon and slipped out the back way. He hurried down the mountain track, casting anxious glances over his shoulder in case anyone spotted him. As soon as he reached the sheltering branches of Witchway Wood, he made for a quiet glade that only he knew about. There, he removed his Hat of Mystery, his Robe of Knowledge and his Cloak of Darkness. Then, clad only in shorts, sandals and socks, he took the egg from his pocket, carefully placed it in the spoon and tried running.

It wasn't as easy as he had hoped. He had had visions of streaking along like a gazelle, arm triumphantly extended before him, egg snugly lodged in the spoon, miles ahead of everybody else and reaching the finish line to thunderous applause. That was until he tried doing it.

The trouble was the egg. Well, the egg and the spoon. Well, the egg, the spoon and the trembling hand. And the feet. And the shorts. The fact was that he couldn't keep the egg steady and see what his feet were doing at the same time. Plus his shorts kept drifting downwards, on account of the limp elastic, so he had to use his other hand to keep them up.

He had been practising for days, but still

couldn't get the hang of it. If he took his eye off the egg even for one second, it fell out of the spoon and rolled away under a bush. But if he didn't watch where he put his feet, he invariably fell flat on his face. Speed was out of the question. The best he could manage was a few shuffling paces at a slow crawl before the inevitable happened. It was all very disheartening.

He was on his hands and knees, crawling under a bush looking for the egg for the hundredth time, when Pongwiffy and Sharkadder found him. They had been flying overhead, on their way back from Scott Sinister's holiday retreat when Pongwiffy spotted a flash of yellow below. She pointed it out to Sharkadder, who recognised her nephew in an instant and insisted on flying down to say hello, although Pongwiffy didn't want to.

They alighted in the glade, propped the Brooms against a tree, folded their arms and surveyed Ronald's rear end.

'Well, well,' said Sharkadder. 'It's you, Ronald. Why are you crawling around under a bush? In those hideous shorts?'

'Looking for his brain,' sneered Pongwiffy, who didn't like Ronald.

Ronald crawled out of the bush, egg in hand, and scrambled to his feet, rather red-faced. There they stood, Aunt Sharky and her horrible friend, staring hard and making him feel self-conscious with his skinny legs and everything.

'Hello, Aunty,' said Ronald unhappily. 'Lovely to see you.'

'Is it?' said Sharkadder. '*Is* it indeed? Well, I'm glad you said that, because I was beginning to think you'd forgotten all about me.'

'I've been a bit busy,' said Ronald, squirming a bit.

'I don't recall getting a thank you letter for the money I sent you for your birthday.'

'I didn't have a stamp.'

'I see. Too busy to walk to the post office.'

'Well . . . yes, actually. I'm in training, you see. For the O'Lumpicks.'

'You're having a joke,' said Pongwiffy. 'You? Entering the O'Lumpicks? *You?*'

'I don't see why not,' said Ronald sulkily. 'It's open to all.'

'I don't remember seeing an entry form for the Wizards,' said Pongwiffy, adding, 'Not that I was looking hard. Wizards and Sport. It's ridiculous, isn't it? I mean, they'd actually have to *move*. If it was a Sitting-In-An-Armchair-Looking-Beardy-And-Eating-Sausages Contest, that'd be different.'

'Now then, Pong,' scolded Sharkadder. 'That's not in the O'Lumpick spirit. You're not allowed to be mean to Ronald. *I* am, but I'm his aunty.'

'Actually,' admitted Ronald, 'actually, it's just me.'

'What—*Team Ronald*?' Pongwiffy guffawed rudely. 'I take it you're going in for the Egg and Spoon? Or is that your lunch?'

'As a matter of fact, I am.'

'Well, you can forget it because the form hasn't arrived. You're not allowed to be in the O'Lumpicks unless you've filled in the form, isn't that right, Sharky?'

Sharkadder hesitated. Rules were rules, but Ronald was family when all was said and done.

'It's in the post,' said Ronald anxiously.

'So you found a stamp for *that*, then?'

151

'It was my last one.'

'Too late,' said Pongwiffy ruthlessly. 'I've told Scott there aren't any Wizards, so he won't have a rhyme for you when he's doing the commentary. And anyway, we don't want thirteen teams, it's unlucky.'

Ronald looked stricken. He looked down at his egg.

'But I've been practising. Aunty, tell her.'

'Try that again. Not forgetting that simple little word.'

'Tell her, *please*. And thank you very much for the money. I'm saving it to buy you a big box of chocolates.'

'No chocolates,' said Sharkadder. 'You don't win sack races on chocolate.'

'Flowers, then.'

Sharkadder relented.

'Oh, I suppose so. We might as well let him, Pong. We're supposed to be intermingling, aren't we?'

'There are limits, though,' said Pongwiffy.

In the end, she agreed that Ronald could enter if his form arrived. It wouldn't do to appear to be a bad sport.

*   *   *

It had been a busy day, and Pongwiffy had had enough. She accepted Sharkadder's invitation to come back to her cottage for a healthy snack and a cup of water. After all that organising, she felt she deserved to put her feet up.

She sat on a comfy chair and idly switched on the spellovision while Sharkadder bustled around

152

the kitchen preparing a bowl of prune and beetroot puree with a small jug of vinegar on the side.

The screen flickered into life. A short plump Genie stood before the palace gates, holding a microphone.

'. . . and behind these gates, even as I speak, the O'Lumpick stadium is being prepared by a hard-working team of Familiars. We had hoped to bring you footage, but it's rather dangerous in there at the moment, with all the tree felling. Unfortunately, King Futtout is unavailable for comment, but I have with me Hugo the Hamster. Hugo, how's it all going?'

The camera zoomed dizzyingly down and homed in on Hugo, holding a clipboard and looking businesslike with a tiny hard hat on his head.

'Ah,' said Pongwiffy. 'Look at him. Sharky, come and look at my Hugo on the spello!'

'What about Dudley?' cried Sharkadder. 'Is he there too?'

'Well, no. He's inside the grounds, digging up rose bushes. Or he will be if he knows what's good for him.'

'In that case,' said Sharkadder, 'I won't bother.'

'Suit yourself.' Pongwiffy reached forward and turned up the volume. Sadly, she missed what Hugo had to say. He was scuttling off through the gates and the camera was wobbling up again.

'So there you have it,' said the Genie, beaming. 'The O'Lumpicks are on track for next Saturday. You have it direct from the Hamster's mouth. This is Ali Pali, returning you to the studio, where the Thing In The Moonmad T-Shirt Hour is about to begin, with special guest Grandwitch Sourmuddle,

153

who once again will be explaining how she came up with such an unusual idea . . .'

Pongwiffy switched it off.

CHAPTER EIGHTEEN

BIGGER

Plugugly was struggling down the stairs with Philpot. It was as much as he could do to manage it. Big? My, was that baby big! Plugugly could no longer get his arms around Philpot's ever-expanding middle. The only way was to hoist him up on to his back like a sack of potatoes, then bend forward into a low crouch. Even then, Philpot's huge pink feet flopped down, thumping on each stair.

'Hold on tight, Baby Philpot!' gasped Plugugly. 'Soon be down de stairs, don't choke me, dere's a good boy!'

'TEE-HEE,' giggled Philpot. *Thump, thump, thump* went his feet. 'MEDSIN.'

Walking down to the gates to collect Philpot's food remained a daily ritual. Cramming him into his pram was easier now he could sit up. There was more space for his bottom half with the rest of him sticking up in the air. His weight was still a problem, though, and the wheels were buckling badly. The pram wouldn't last much longer.

Philpot shouldn't be sitting up, of course. But as we know, his development is accelerating wildly. He is growing by the hour, not just by the day. He has other talents too. He can now say words (MEDSIN! MORE! 'GAIN! and NO!), has all his teeth and can take notice of things instead of just lying around gnawing his own feet. He is far too advanced for a two-week-old baby.

You will notice that Philpot's baby vocabulary does not include the words MAMA or DADA. This is because Philpot sees very little of his mother and father. Taking full advantage of Nanny Susan, Bigsy and Largette have been going out on long, carefree bike rides, coming home late and sleeping in every day, safe in the knowledge that their offspring is being well cared for by a professional.

Plugugly and Philpot had reached the landing where the Stonkings had their bedroom.

'NANNY SUSAN?' called Largette. 'IS THAT YOU? COULD YOU STEP IN HERE ONE MOMENT? BIGSY AND I WOULD LIKE A WORD.'

Plugugly's ears pricked up. Perhaps they were about to give him his wages. That would be good. Plugugly loved looking after Philpot, but he loved sweeties more. He couldn't wait to stride triumphantly into the cave, waving a big bag of gold! That would be the end of the nannying job, which would be sad, but not *that* sad. He was fond of Philpot, but a ton or two of sweets would certainly help him get over it.

156

'NANNY SUSAN? ARE YOU COMING?'

Plugugly hesitated. He had a dilemma. He couldn't spell it, and didn't know what it meant, but a dilemma was what he had. On the one hand, he wanted his wages. On the other, he didn't want the Stonkings to see Baby Philpot. They hadn't been up to the nursery for days, and Plugugly didn't want them to see him now. Plugugly could no longer be in denial. Even he could see that there was a real problem. And he had a bad feeling that it was all his fault. It was all down to the wrong diet. Plugugly suspected that he might be in trouble if the Stonkings caught a glimpse of their vastly oversized, frighteningly advanced offspring and the truth came out.

Of course, the truth *would* come out eventually. Plugugly couldn't keep Philpot under wraps for ever. But hopefully, by then he would have his bag of gold and would be a safe distance away.

He heaved Philpot off his back and set him on the floor by the stairs, which led steeply down to the hall. There was no rail or baby gate. It was a silly place to leave a baby, but Plugugly's Nanny Susan side wasn't working so well. His true Goblin nature had kicked in. He was thinking about gold and sweets.

He reached into his apron pocket, took out a gigantic dummy and plugged it into Philpot's mouth.

'Wait dere, Baby Philpot,' instructed Plugugly. 'Nanny'll be right back. Will you be good?'

Philpot regarded him solemnly, removed the dummy and said very clearly, ' 'ES.'

Talk about advanced development! He had only been up an hour, but already he could say another word.

'Ahhh,' said Plugugly fondly. 'Dere's Nanny's clever boy.'

Philpot casually replaced his own dummy and sucked contentedly.

Plugugly straightened his bonnet, adjusted his skirts, opened the bedroom door and went in.

Bigsy and Largette's gigantic bed was strewn with clothing. They were busily folding garments and stuffing them into a large motorbike pannier. Both of them were wearing leather jackets, boots and helmets. Largette was wearing a lot of red lipstick. Bigsy had all his gold chains on and was sporting goggles. The floor was awash with Largette's shoes. Hopefully, Plugugly looked around for the bag of gold.

'AH,' said Largette. 'I'M GLAD WE CAUGHT YOU, NANNY SUSAN. WE'RE GOING AWAY FOR A FEW DAYS. JUST A LITTLE BREAK. BIGSY'S TAKING ME BACK TO GIANT TOWN TO VISIT MUM.'

'Oh,' said Plugugly politely. 'Right. What about Baby Philpot? Is you thinkin' of takin' him?'

'NAH,' said Bigsy. 'NOT ON THE BIKE. GOTTA BE RESPONSIBLE.'

'WE THOUGHT HE'D BE BETTER OFF HERE WITH YOU,' explained Largette. 'IT'D SPOIL HIS ROUTINE IF WE TOOK HIM. HE MIGHT START ROARING AGAIN. THEN WHAT WOULD WE DO?'

This may seem odd to us, the Stonkings proposing to whoosh off for the weekend leaving their baby behind. But they are Giants. Giants aren't bothered about babies until they become toddlers. It's tough, but that's the way it is.

'SO WILL THAT BE ALL RIGHT WITH YOU?' asked Largette.

'Oh yes. Dat's all right.'

'YOU'RE A TREASURE. SAY 'BYE TO BABY PHILPOT. LOTS OF KISSES FROM MUMMY AND DADDY. NOW THEN. DID I PACK MY PINK HEELS?'

And that was it. Plugugly left the room. It was only when he got outside that he remembered about the gold. He was about to go back and mention it, when he suddenly realised something.

Philpot was gone! He had been propped up against the wall, sucking his dummy, and now he wasn't there!

Plugugly's jaw dropped. Oh *no*!

Could he have toppled over and fallen down the stairs? Surely that would have made a big crash? Not necessarily. Not if he rolled down. But he might have bumped his precious huge head on the banisters . . .

Heart in his mouth, Plugugly approached the top of the stairs and looked down.

Philpot was indeed downstairs. He hadn't fallen, though. He had crawled.

Right now, he was halfway across the tiled hallway, be-nappied big bottom in the air, heading for the front door. Considering he was on his hands and knees, he had a fair turn of speed.

Greatly relieved, Plugugly picked up his skirts and hurried down to rescue him.

So. Baby Philpot has reached the next important stage. He is mobile. This will be even more difficult.

159

CHAPTER NINETEEN

ONE DAY TO GO

It was the day before the O'Lumpicks. All over Witchway Wood, the teams of dedicated athletes were getting in those final, critical hours of practice. Even before the sun rose, the place was awash with grim-faced joggers. Every glade was commandeered by determined-looking weight-lifters. Everywhere you looked, there were sack racers and egg-and-spooners and high jumpers and relay teams clutching batons.

Every so often, from somewhere in the Wood, there would come a resounding, faraway crash. That was Macabre, practising Tossing the Caber. Even the Trolls had declined to enter for that event, because whatever a Caber was, tossing it sounded dangerous. Macabre was the sole competitor, so she was certain of winning a gold medal. The trouble was, tossing a large, sharpened tree trunk was proving surprisingly tricky. It still landed on her own foot more often than she would like. But Macabre had her pride. She didn't want to make a complete fool of herself. Anyway, the exercise was doing her good.

Three whole weeks of healthy eating and vigorous activity had transformed the residents of the Wood. Mind you, they had paid the price. There were strained muscles, scabby knees and sprained ankles in evidence. There was quite a bit of under-the-breath moaning. Yes, all the teams were highly excited about the O'Lumpicks and determined to do their very best and win all the medals whilst remaining suitably humble and unfailingly polite to fellow competitors, which was in the rules. But getting fit had been *hard*. The noble athletes were getting a bit fed up with it now. They were looking forward to when it was all over and they could go back to normal. Slob around on the sofa with a big *Bog Bar* and a bag of *Hoppy Jumpers*, boasting loudly about their sporting achievements. Of course, nobody admitted this. It didn't go with the O'Lumpick spirit.

Everyone was practising intermingling too, because the rules stated that it was compulsory. This was proving a strain. Instead of ignoring each other, there were tight-lipped smiles and polite little waves and the odd courtly bow. The Ghoulish relay team politely gave way for a clutch of jogging Skeletons. A sprinting Vampire offered the twins a sip of his water. Instead of laughing in his face, they said thank you and waited until he had run off before spitting it out behind a bush.

Egg and Spoon athletes stood aside for Sack athletes, even though their instinct was to trip them up. A weightlifting Zombie put down his rock and gallantly came to Sharkadder's aid. (She insisted on wearing high heels when practising for the Sack Race and kept skewering herself into the ground.) Bendyshanks gave a passing Banshee one of her apples. It looked a bit wormy, but it was still quite nice of her. There was even the occasional insincere cry of 'Good luck!' or 'May the best team win!'

As well as all the sporting activity, there were lots of other things going on. Finishing touches were being added to flags. Parade costumes were being tried on. Shorts were being washed and ironed. The spellovision crew noisily staked out King Futtout's gardens, deciding where they should set up their equipment and accidentally setting fire to his shed, which caused a bit of drama.

In the Wizards' Clubhouse, Ronald was in his room in the process of sneakily glueing an egg into a spoon. Despite all that practice, he was still hopeless. Cheating was the only way to win. This was shocking, of course. He should have read the rules on the entry form. Although even if he had, I'm sorry to say he still would have done it.

King Futtout was in his treasury, also up to his armpits in glue. He was attempting to stick some of Honeydimple's red hair ribbons on to a number of gold, silver and copper coins that he hoped would do for the medals he'd been ordered to provide. Earlier in the day, Queen Beryl and Princess Honeydimple had taken the royal coach and departed in a furious cloud of dust, leaving him on his own. Honeydimple would make a fuss about the ribbons when she got back, but right now he was past caring.

163

Scott Sinister stood before a full-length mirror, practising his commentary.

'So! Here they come, the Witches' team
With vibrant costumes all a-gleam.
The fittest Witches in the land.
Stand up and give them a big hand.
I have to say they look so fine
I'm giving them an extra line
And a half.
And now, behold the Troll brigade
Who round the ground do now parade . . .'

Yes. It was all go in Witchway Wood—and nobody was busier than Pongwiffy. There were so many last-minute things to do.

She began by inspecting the stadium.

King Futtout's lovely gardens had been . . . well, transformed isn't quite the word. Ruined, more like. There was a newly built podium at one end, where the gazebo used to be. Miles of tangled bunting was suspended between the few trees that hadn't been chopped down. Rows of chairs were set around the edges, where the crowds from far and wide would sit. The lawn was a riot of wiggly, wobbly white lines. In one corner, two rickety poles had been set up next to a sign declaring High Jump. An area had been set aside for the Weightlifting. Several rocks of varying size and weight lay in a dangerous pile, ready to be hefted. Bushes had been uprooted and left in a careless pile behind the King's slightly charred shed, which was being used to store the Witches' Parade costumes.

After three weeks of ferocious sewing machine activity, Sharkadder had finally unveiled her handiwork. The costumes consisted of thirteen

164

flowing cloaks in a wide variety of clashing colours. Each cloak had a sparkling hem, because she had gone seriously mad with glitter. Each had a matching pointy hat with a tassel and a matching pair of shorts. Sharkadder was thrilled with her efforts. Nobody else was quite so sure, but they didn't like to say so.

She spotted Pongwiffy running around setting out more chairs and made her come in and try on her costume. To Pongwiffy's horror, it was all white. The hat stood tall, white and pointy, not at all like the battered, floppy, comfortable one she always wore. The shorts looked ridiculous.

'White?' said Pongwiffy, staring down. '*WHITE*?'

'Don't you like it?' asked Sharkadder, sounding hurt. 'I made yours especially nice, as you're leading the Parade. I wanted you to look your best. I thought you'd like it.'

'But *white*. It's just not me. Don't you have anything in dirt?'

'There's no such colour as dirt.'

'What d'you call my cardigan, then?'

'I'd call it disgusting. But if you *really* want to spoil the Parade and let everyone down after I've spent all this time . . .'

'No, no. Keep your hair on. I suppose I'll get used to it. Anyway, I can't stop, I've got a million things to do. I don't suppose you want to help arrange the chairs? Or set out the programmes? Or anything?'

'I can't. I've got to hang up the costumes, then put in a few more hours' practice with the sack. You want me to win, don't you?'

'Nggh,' said Pongwiffy, which could have meant

anything.

And off she went, leaving Sharkadder to pick up the offending cloak, hat and matching shorts from the floor.

And so the day wore on, until the sun dropped below the horizon and the stars came out. At that point, everyone went home to eat a last healthy supper, do a few last exercises, then fall exhaustedly into bed for a last, sensible early night. Tomorrow was the Witchway Wood O'Lumpick Games. They had put in the effort, and tomorrow they would find out whether it had been worth it. But now, they could do no more.

*   *   *

'Phew!' sighed Pongwiffy. She was in Number One, Dump Edge, lying flat on her sofa with a cold flannel on her head and her feet up. 'What a day. I can't be bothered to do exercises.'

'Got to exercise,' scolded Hugo. He was over in the corner with a tiny set of dumb-bells. As far as he was concerned, the Weightlifting medal was in the bag. 'Every night, every mornink. Like me. Last chance, tomorrow ze Big Day.'

'But I'm not competing. What's the point?'

'Duzzn't matter. You vant to stay fit, ya? So do exercises.'

'No. Leave me alone. I'll just have supper and turn in.'

'OK,' sighed Hugo with a little shrug. 'You ze boss. I get you nice bowl of radishes.'

'What, the ones Sharkadder sent round? The ones in lime jelly with a dollop of mustard on the top?'

166

'Ya.'

'Is that all there is?'

'Pretty well.'

'Well, I don't want them. I'm fed up with vegetables, particularly Sharkadder's. What I want is a big, greasy bowl of skunk stew. There, I've said it. And don't bother to tell me off because I don't care.'

Pongwiffy pulled a cushion over her face and lapsed into silence.

'Mistress?' said Hugo.

'What?'

'Sumsink ze matter?'

'Yes,' growled Pongwiffy, her voice muffled because of the cushion. 'As a matter of fact, there is. I'm fed up with the O'Lumpicks. In fact, I wish I'd never suggested them. I thought they'd be fun. That's what *you* said. But I haven't had any fun at all so far. It's been all work, work, work. And horrible food.'

'But zat good for you. Hard work, healthy food.'

'Yes, well, you can have too much of a good thing.'

'But is vorking! Look how much you change. Better colour. Not so creaky. I look at you now, I don't see old Pongviffy. I see new.'

'Old or new, I still ended up running the whole thing by myself. I'm worn out. Too much to do and no one to help.'

'Vot about ze Sports Committee?'

'What Sports Committee? They're all too busy practising for their event. They've gone all competitive. All they care about is winning medals.'

'Vell, ya. Athletes got to take Sport seriously,'

said Hugo, flexing his tiny, iron-hard muscles.

'So I gather. You Familiars haven't exactly pitched in lately, have you? Even Greymatter's given up pretending to help. She just handed me a million lists and went off to practise the stupid Relay. And Sharky just leaps away in her sack whenever she sees me, then sends round more horrible food to poison me. I'm the only one not *in* anything, so it's left to me to organise where the coaches will park and where the crowds from far and wide will sit and where Scott's going to stand. And find him a megaphone, and put a glass of water on his podium. And decide where the Rhythm Boys and the television crew will set up and explain to Futtout how to judge. It's all too much and I'm sick of it. You'd think someone would say thank you, but no one ever does.'

'*I* do,' said Hugo kindly. '*I* say sank you.'

'Yes, but you're my Familiar. You've got to.'

'Cheer up,' said Hugo. 'You get to lead ze Grand Opening Parade, remember? Get to hold ze flag. Big honour.'

'Well, yes, I know that. And I was quite keen to start with. Until I saw my costume.'

'Vot it like?'

'White. I think Sharky hates me.'

'No, she don't,' soothed Hugo. 'You vant to know secret?'

'Yes. What?'

'She got Scott to make up special poem. For you. He goink to say nice sings. He goink to sank you for 'elping to make ze day so vunderful. He goink to read it out at ze end. You take special bow. Everybody give you big clap. Big close-up on ze spellovision.'

'Really?' Pongwiffy removed the pillow from her face.

'Ya. I hear zis from Dudley. He say not to tell you. Is s'posed to be surprise.'

'A special poem, eh?' Pongwiffy cheered up a bit. 'Well, that's different. Perhaps I'll get presented with an organiser medal. I wonder if anyone's organised that? If I'd known earlier, I'd have done it myself.' She gave a huge yawn. 'Oh well, too late now. I'm going to bed. Have to be up at the crack of dawn tomorrow. It's starting at ten, but the coaches will begin arriving long before that. I have to be there to greet Scott and put Futtout in place and make sure everything's ready.'

'You vant I get up, give you breakfast?'

'Would that be radishes in jelly, by any chance?'

'Funny you should say zat.'

Pongwiffy gave a heavy sigh. What she really fancied was a big, greasy fry-up, followed by one of Hugo's home-made cakes. But those days were long gone.

CHAPTER TWENTY

PHILPOT WALKS!

Time now to catch up on developments at Stonking Towers.

Several days have passed since Philpot's loving parents roared off into the blue. For Giant babies, particularly an advanced one who has been prematurely weaned on unsuitable solids, even one day is a long time. The phrase 'My! How he's grown!' in no way does him justice.

Philpot hasn't just grown. He has expanded, like the universe. He has shot up, spread, widened, heightened, broadened and thoroughly enlarged. The crib cannot hold him. The pram cannot hold him.

Philpot is HUGE. He now towers over Plugugly, who has long given up trying to carry him. So it's just as well that he can now walk. Well, lurch. It's not so much walking as unsteady lurching, interspersed with intervals of mad, staggery running.

He can talk too. Not just DIN DIN, and NO and 'GAIN and 'ES. He can say WANT GO WALKIES. He can say MORE MEDSIN PEES TANK OO. He refers to himself as 'POT, which is cute. He can say 'POT LOVE NANA SU-SU, which makes Plugugly almost weep with pleasure.

Mind you, it's no picnic. Keeping Philpot happy is a full-time job. Because his crib is too small, he now sleeps in Plugugly's bed with Plugugly, which is horrible. Plugugly spends all night hanging over the edge while Philpot blissfully slumbers on. During the day, Philpot is wildly energetic. His diet needs a lot of working off. He is constantly on the go, falling downstairs and bumping his head, crying a bit and needing to be soothed. Then off again to run full tilt at the front door and get poked in the eye by the door knob.

Somehow, though, Plugugly is coping. He plays peek-a-boo, which makes Philpot laugh. He feeds him and baths him. He can be strict too. If Philpot *really* misbehaves, he has to sit on the naughty step.

Plugugly has taken to going for long walks in the Wood with Philpot toddling happily along beside him, reined in by a piece of string attached to his nappy with a safety pin. Plugugly doesn't really enjoy these walks, because he's so exhausted he can hardly keep his eyes open. But walking is the only way to wear Philpot out. Philpot always goes to sleep on the way back, and has to be dragged up the steps and through the front door by his feet. Plugugly tiptoes away, leaving him snoozing on the doormat in the hall. It's the only time he can catch forty winks for himself.

Despite it all, they are getting on all right. After

horrifying bath times, when Philpot thrashes around flooding the bathroom, giggling merrily whilst bashing Plugugly over the head with a giant plastic duck, he suddenly becomes all loving. He cuddles up in his big white towel, pats Plugugly's cheek and says, ' 'POT LOVE NANA SU-SU.' That always makes Plugugly's heart melt, although he is half drowned. Then comes the uncomfortable night, morning time, nappy changing, breakfast, then another walk. That is the routine.

The two of them are on one of these long walks right now.

'No, Baby Philpot,' said Plugugly. Philpot was straining sideways at the leash. He had seen a quicksand he always liked to fall in. He had done it two days running and each time Plugugly had had to fish him out. 'We's not stoppin' dere, you'll get all mucky again.'

Philpot stuck out his bottom lip. The swamp called to him. He *wanted* to fall in. Tears welled in his eyes.

'If you is a good boy Nanny'll give you extra medicine when we goes home,' promised Plugugly. 'Now, stay on de parf, dere's a dear.'

Philpot brightened up. He didn't stay cross for long, especially if medicine was promised. Anyway, despite his size he had the attention span of a gnat.

'MEDSIN PEES TANK OO,' he agreed.

Something caught his eye ahead, and he waved a massive dimpled arm and went charging off, yanking Plugugly behind him by his string.

'Slow down, Baby Philpot!' begged Plugugly. 'Nanny Susan can't keep up!'

The thing that had caught Philpot's attention was a flag. A small, red, triangular flag, hanging

173

limply over the branch of a tree. (In fact, this had blown off the bunting that right now was adorning the O'Lumpick stadium, although neither Philpot nor Plugugly knew this.)

Philpot liked the look of the flag. He toddled up, reached out, plucked it from the tree and flapped it about.

'PITTY!' he roared. 'PITTY!'

'Dat's right,' gasped Plugugly, screeching to a halt. 'It *is* pretty, Baby Philpot. You play wiv de pretty flag while Nanny sits down for a minute.'

Scarlet in the face, he sank on to a nearby tree trunk and mopped his sweating brow.

'FLAG!' bellowed Philpot, his vocabulary swelling by the second. 'PITTY FLAG, TEE HEE!'

'Dat's it, you wave it, dat's de way.'

Philpot experimentally put the flag in his mouth. No. It didn't taste nice. He flapped it about a bit more, then put it on his head. He had a feeling it was a funny thing to do. Sometimes, Nanny Susan put things on her head, to make him laugh. He especially liked it when she did it with his plastic bath duck.

'LOOKA!' he demanded. 'LOOKA, NANA SU-SU.'

But his request wasn't met. Plugugly had toppled off the tree trunk and was lying flat out on the leafy ground, fast asleep.

'NANA SU-SU?' enquired Philpot. He toddled up to Plugugly and gave him an experimental pat on the cheek. No response. Philpot looked down at Plugugly's hand. The hand that held the end of his restraining string. Philpot reached down and one by one, bent back Plugugly's unresisting fingers.

174

The string slithered out. Plugugly didn't stir.

'PEEK-A-BOO?' said Philpot. Still no response.

'MEDSIN PEES TANK OO?' tried Philpot hopefully. But no medicine was forthcoming.

Philpot stared around. This was getting boring. Nanny Susan clearly didn't want to play. What should he do?

'WALKIES,' announced Philpot to himself.

And he set off into the trees, trailing his leash behind him.

* * *

Some time later, the Goblins were lying around the cave doing nothing in particular when the front boulder rolled open with a crash. There stood Plugugly, bonnet askew, eyes bulging, wringing his hands, beside himself with anxiety.

'He's gone!' wailed Plugugly. 'I's lost him, he's gone. Oh, oh, whatever shall I do?'

'Wha—? Who's gone?' enquired Lardo, opening one eye. He had been having a little snooze and didn't like being so rudely awakened.

'Baby Philpot! I was takin' him for his walk an' I musta dropped off an' now he's gone!'

'Ah, but 'ave you got the gold, though?' asked Stinkwart uncaringly.

'No! I hasn't got paid yet! Dey've gone away but dey're comin' back soon an' dey'll want to know where he is an' I don't *know*!' howled Plugugly, hopping from one foot to the other in a frenzy of panic.

'So you still ain't got the gold? After waitin' all this time for you to come back wiv it so we can go an' buy sweeties, now you're tellin' us . . .'

'Stop goin' on about *gold*!' roared Plugugly. 'Baby Philpot's lost in de woods an' all you can fink about is *gold*!'

'Ain't my fault he's lost,' argued Stinkwart. 'You're the nanny, aintcha?'

'Stinkwart's right,' agreed Hog. 'We spends all that time gettin' you kitted out an' sits around waitin' for you to come back wiv the gold an' then you goes and loses 'im. So don't go blamin' us.'

'I cannot believe dis!' gasped Plugugly. 'Dis is a *baby* we is talkin' about. Suppose he falls in a bog? Or gets eated by bears? Anyfin' could happen. What am I s'posed to tell his mummy an' daddy when dey gets back?'

'Tell 'em they owes you a bag o' gold,' suggested Sproggit.

'Is you *mad*?' cried Plugugly. 'Does you really fink dey'll pay up when dey finds out I've *lost de baby*?'

A little silence fell while the Goblins considered this.

'No,' said Slopbucket at length. 'I s'pose they won't.'

'Dere you are, den! Anyway, it's not about de money, it's about findin' Baby Philpot before somefin' bad happens to him.'

'Off you go, then,' said Sproggit. 'Let us know how you get on.'

'*Me?* I can't do it on my own, can I? We has got to form a search party. Come on, come on, don't just sit dere!'

Grumbling, the Goblins climbed to their feet, set their hats straight and left the cave to go baby hunting.

CHAPTER TWENTY-ONE

A CRAAASH!

It was the morning of the O'Lumpicks, and Pongwiffy rose at dawn. Despite an early night, she hadn't slept well. There had been a lot of nightmares, all based on the forthcoming day and the things that might go wrong. She had dreamed that Scott Sinister had backed out at the last minute, that King Futtout had sailed off to sea with the medals, that the Witches had come last in every single event and, worst of all, that she had tripped over and dropped the flag, making herself a laughing stock, and been thrown out of the Coven by Sourmuddle, who for some reason was wearing a gorilla suit and carrying a tennis racquet. Sadly, there was no special poem or organiser medal in her dreams.

There had been strange noises out in the Wood too. Even when in the middle of bad dreams, Pongwiffy always had one ear open. There were distant crashings and weird, despairing cries. *Baaaby Fiiilll Pot!* That's what it sounded like. She hadn't a clue what that was all about, but it certainly hadn't made for a good night's sleep.

When the first light filtered through the hovel window, she climbed out of bed, thought about touching her toes, didn't, and reached for her boots. Pongwiffy always slept in her clothes because it saved time, but since the new fitness regime she had taken to removing her boots in order to give her socks room to breathe.

Boots on, she glanced across at Hugo, who was snoring heavily in the tea cosy he used for a bed. His little set of dumb-bells was placed within reach. Should she wake him? No. It was going to be a big day for him. He needed all the sleep he could get. Ratsnappy was the Witches' Weightlifter, and of course, Pongwiffy was hoping that she would do well, but secretly she wanted Hugo to win the gold after all the effort he had put into training.

Anyway, quite frankly, she wasn't in the mood for breakfast. The thought of the day ahead was making her tummy churn in a very unpleasant way. Of course, there was the specially commissioned poem to look forward to, but there was a lot to get through before she could enjoy her moment of glory. Best to take a brisk stroll along to the palace and make sure that everything was in place before anyone else arrived.

She found a scrap of paper and a pencil, wrote *gon to staddium gud luk* and left it on the kitchen table. Then she tiptoed out.

It was still quite dark as she walked through the Wood. It was deathly silent too, which is why she gave such a start when she heard the noise.

CRAAAAASH!

It was the sound of breaking glass. An almighty smash, followed by a hail of tinkling. It caused her to nearly jump out of her boots. Startled birds took off from the treetops. What on *earth* could it be? Pongwiffy hadn't been there for ages, but she felt sure it came from the direction of *Sugary Candy's*.

Heart pounding, she moved through the trees. She felt slightly nervous, but curiosity had got the better of her. Had the Yetis finally come to tear the shop down? Nobody had seen them for ages. Perhaps they had decided to collect all their unwanted stock, which she had heard was still on display behind the unbreakable window.

When she reached the glade, she could hardly believe her eyes. The crash had come from *Sugary Candy's* all right. But there was no sign of the Yetis.

Where the unbreakable window had been, there was a great, gaping hole. Millions of glass shards lay before it on the ground. And inside . . . inside, in the shadowy darkness, something . . . no, *somebody* . . . was moving around. An enormous shape.

'Hello?' called Pongwiffy. 'Who's there?'

Silence.

She wished she had her Wand. All magical aids were banned from the O'Lumpicks, so she had dutifully left it under her pillow. But something interesting was going on, and she was burning to know what.

Cautiously, she left the shelter of the bushes and crept towards the shattered window, broken glass grinding under her boots. Heart in her mouth, she

179

peered inside. What she saw made her go weak at the knees.

Standing in the middle of the shop, in a sea of glass shards and spilled sweets, was—*a Giant baby!* A Giant baby, wearing nothing but a big, droopy nappy and a huge, face-splitting grin. The soles of its enormous, bare pink feet must have been as tough as leather, because the glass didn't seem to bother it in the slightest. A long piece of string was attached to its nappy with a safety pin.

'DIN-DIN,' said the Giant baby, catching sight of Pongwiffy. It gave a delighted little giggle, and waved a huge, fat arm. 'TEE HEE! DIN-DIN!'

'What?' said Pongwiffy.

'DIN-DIN,' explained Philpot patiently.

He stooped down, scooped up a handful of red sweets shaped like little lips, crammed them into his mouth, slurped and added, 'MMMM.'

Pongwiffy didn't know what to do. It wasn't a situation she had come across before. She just stood hovering before the collapsed window, trying to make sense of it. A gigantic baby had broken the unbreakable window of *Sugary Candy's*, and was happily helping himself to free sweets. Who was he? She hadn't a clue. Where had he come from? Likewise. Where were his parents? Not around, hopefully. What should she do about it? Well, considering his size, probably nothing.

The Giant baby crunched and slurped. Sticky red goo ran from his mouth. Very suddenly, he sat down with a loud bump and began casting about for more sweets. He shovelled up two more fistfuls—a deliciously sticky, multicoloured mixture of *Minty Stingeroos*, *Beezi Kneezies* and *Wizard Wobblers*—and rammed them in his

180

cavernous mouth.

'YUM,' said Philpot appreciatively. He crunched, swallowed and waved his huge arms around, pointing excitedly to the surrounding feast. 'GA?'

'What?' said Pongwiffy again. She wasn't used to babies.

'GA!' shouted Philpot. 'GA!'

'I don't quite get you,' said Pongwiffy. 'Could you be a little more explicit?'

'GA! DIN-DIN!'

'Well, yes,' agreed Pongwiffy. 'Yes, I suppose it is.'

Philpot's excited eye caught sight of a toppled mountain of broken chocolate bars. He rolled over on to his knees and took off in a jet-propelled crawl. Crushed sweets and broken glass did nothing to slow him down. He was possessed.

Pongwiffy watched him eat. The expression on his brown smeared face was blissful. Never was there a happier baby. Huge though he was, he certainly seemed friendly enough. He spotted Pongwiffy staring and gave her a rather sweet little wave.

'DIN-DIN?' he said again.

It was almost as though he was inviting her to join him.

Pongwiffy gazed around. Her shock at coming face to face with a Giant baby was ebbing away, particularly as he seemed so amenable. Her brain was slowly starting to work again. Thoughts began to form. Not particularly good thoughts, I'm afraid, but we're dealing with Pongwiffy here. Here are her thoughts, for the record.

Sugary Candy's window had finally met its match.

Magic hadn't touched it, battering rams hadn't cracked it, hurled rocks hadn't dented the surface. But a Giant baby had arrived from nowhere and done what no one else had managed to do. How? Who knows. Probably just kicked it in, with bare feet. And now the place was awash with mouth-watering free sweets. *Free sweets!* After three weeks of munching on raw carrots. And not everything was on the floor. Some of the jars, the ones on the back shelves, remained intact. There was nobody around, apart from the baby. The O'Lumpicks wouldn't be starting for ages. She had plenty of time. It was oh so tempting. Perhaps just one, eh? One little sweet wouldn't hurt anybody. She deserved it, didn't she? A little reward for working so hard.

Briskly, she stepped through the window. She edged around the Giant baby, who was experimenting with how many lollies he could fit in his mouth at one time. (Thirteen.) She stepped over a mountain of spilled *Minty Stingeroos*, waded through a small desert of sherbet, marched around the counter, reached up to the top shelf, took down a jar of *Hoppy Jumpers* and unscrewed the cap.

'Here,' she said. 'Hold your hands out. Try some of these. They're lovely.'

'TANK OO!' said Philpot, just as Nanny Susan had taught him to say.

'You're welcome,' said Pongwiffy. And popped one in her mouth.

CHAPTER TWENTY-TWO

THE O'LUMPICKS

The sun shone brightly and a warm breeze blew across the stadium which was rapidly filling up. The long queue at the palace gates was getting shorter as excited spectators took their places and the various teams of noble athletes scurried around looking for places where they could change into their outfits for the Grand Opening Parade. The place was a hive of activity.

King Futtout drooped miserably in his best throne, which had been carted out of the palace and set at the end of the lawn, right by the finishing line. In one limp hand was a list of all the Games, with spaces to write the names of the winners. In the other limp hand was a pencil. Placed on a small table next to him was a box containing his home-made medals. Despite his best efforts, they hadn't turned out too well.

His tragic eyes surveyed the wreckage of his

once lovely garden. Absent trees. Missing rose bushes. Wiggly white lines all over the lawn. A large podium where his gazebo used to be. A pile of boulders for the Weightlifting. A mound of sacks, a bucket of eggs, a collection of spoons and bundles of ropes. His washing line commandeered for the High Jump. Miles of tacky bunting. Rows of mismatched chairs, some from Witchway Hall and others pinched from his own palace. Chairs which seated the crowds from far and wide, some of whom had arrived a good hour or so earlier in ramshackle coaches which were even now cluttering up the palace coach yard.

They were a mixed bunch, the crowds from far and wide, consisting mainly of the various teams' families and friends. A lot of them sported cameras and picnic baskets. Flags on sticks and silly hats emblazoned with the teams' names were much in evidence. Sadly, there wasn't much mingling going on. The different factions tended to sit with their own kind. However, they weren't fighting either. Everyone knew about the good sportsmanship rule. No one wanted to let the side down.

You will be pleased to know that the Witches had supporters. Two, to be precise. Pierre de Gingerbeard, the famous Dwarf chef who happens to be Sharkadder's cousin, was there. He was sitting next to his brother, Wildman Willy Racoon, Sharkadder's other cousin, who is a famous wild man from the mountains. Both sported *Go Witches!* badges. That was all, but Witches don't have many friends. They were lucky to get two.

The spellovision crew had arrived and were getting their camera and microphones organised.

186

On the bandstand, the Rhythm Boys were tuning up. Filth revved up with a particularly violent drum thrash, causing King Futtout to wince and clutch his head.

'No sleeping on the job, Futtout,' said a voice in his ear. Grandwitch Sourmuddle was standing next to him, wearing a bright orange cloak with matching hat. She had declined to wear shorts, declaring that they weren't a Grandwitch sort of thing. Snoop stood at her side, holding a large watch.

'I wasn't,' said King Futtout miserably. 'I'm . . . erm . . . just wondering what my wife is going to say.'

'Oh, she'll get over it. I hope you're going to sit up straighter than that when we get started. Which we will, as soon as Scott Sinister arrives. Which he's supposed to, any minute. And Pongwiffy, of course.'

'I think he's here,' said Snoop, pointing at the palace gates, where a long, low coach was drawing up, pulled by a team of coal black horses. The number plate read SS1. Scott liked to arrive in style. The coachman jumped down and opened the door with a flourish. Cameras flashed as the great man stepped out, swishing his gold and scarlet cloak and flashing his trademark sunglasses. He was holding a monogrammed briefcase, which contained his poetic commentary. A surge of fans rushed up clamouring for autographs and a teenage girl Troll fainted.

'Where is he supposed to stand?' wondered Sourmuddle. 'What do we do with him? Pongwiffy's supposed to be dealing with this. Oh, where *is* she? She promised to be here to greet him.'

'She's late,' tutted Snoop. 'Very, *very* late.'

'You don't need to tell me that, Snoop. The whole Coven was relying on her to get here early. If it wasn't the O'Lumpicks, I'd give her ten millionple black marks. Sadly I can't, because I've got to be a good sport. Where's Hugo?'

'With the Familiars, behind the bandstand. They're arguing about their flag.'

'Well, have you asked him where she is?'

Snoop shrugged. 'He hasn't a clue. She left early this morning and he hasn't seen her since.'

'Well, she'd better turn up soon. We can't start without her. Go and round up all the teams. We need to kick off the second she arrives.'

Snoop went off to do as he was told.

Macabre came marching up. She was dressed from head to foot in tartan, liberally sprinkled with glitter. It was an odd combination, particularly the shorts. Sharkadder had got the measurements a bit wrong and they ended at her ankles, in effect making them not so much shorts as longs. In her hand was a furled flag.

'What's happening?' demanded Macabre. 'We're supposed tay be starting the Parade as soon as that film star gets his act together.'

'Well, we can't, can we?' snapped Sourmuddle. 'Pongwiffy's not here. We'll have to get Scott to stall. I said she could lead us in, remember? A promise is a promise.'

'Since when?'

'Since now,' said Sourmuddle firmly. 'The O'Lumpicks are all about being honourable and fair. I've been on spello explaining about it for weeks. Stop looking so grouchy, it's only for today.'

'Mmm. Well, all I know is she'd better not see me tomorrow.'

'Me neither,' agreed Sourmuddle darkly.

'Erm . . . excuse me?' bleated King Futtout. 'I think the um . . . film star needs some attention. He's looking a little put out.'

He pointed limply to where Scott Sinister was waving away Sharkadder, radiant in vibrant turquoise, who was attempting to manhandle him on to the podium. Scott was objecting because nobody had thought to provide him with a glass of fizzy water. Sourmuddle and Macabre hurried off to help, leaving King Futtout alone and ignored on his throne.

Behind the bandstand, Snoop was getting the teams lined up. It would take too long to describe them all in detail, but here's a quick summary of how they look. It's worth it, because they all had a very different take on what constitutes the perfect Grand Opening Parade outfit.

The Skeletons are in crisp white shorts and black bow ties. The Trolls have gone in for furry loincloths. The Zombies are in tight-fitting suits with half mast trousers. The Mummies (only two in their team) are in their usual bandages, with the unusual addition of top hats. The Ghosts are in traditional white sheets. The Ghouls are mainly in rags, but they've washed and ironed them. The Gnomes (including GNorman, who is entering for the Sack Race) are in little red pointy hats and green trousers. The Vampires are in black cloaks lined with scarlet, and smell strongly of toothpaste. The Banshees are in their best nighties, and weeping already at the thought that they might not win. The Familiars are all different shapes, sizes and species, so they haven't bothered to dress up in anything special. That's why they've put so much thought into their flag, which even at this late stage is causing dissent. They've finally gone with Vernon's black letters on a white sheet idea, but none of the Cats are happy.

There are two teams with only one member. These are the time-wasting Werewolf, wearing his best trousers and brandishing a relay baton, and Ronald in his yellow shorts, trying not to look guilty about what is in his pocket. (An egg glued to a spoon. Tut tut.)

Lining up first are the Witches in their technicolour cloaks, hats and matching shorts. In terms of vibrancy, they have certainly won the day, although it hurts your eyes to look at them.

The Familiars came next. Snoop scuttled up to give them their last minute instructions.

'Have you all got your flags ready?' he enquired. Nervous nods all round. 'Well, keep them furled until it's your turn to march in.'

'How do we know when that is?' asked Barry the Vulture.

'Just listen out for your poem. Mr Sinister's written some special verses in honour of the occasion. The minute you hear your name, you're on. He'll say a few words first, though. We're playing for time because Pongwiffy still hasn't arrived.'

Everyone turned and looked enquiringly at Hugo, who shrugged and mumbled, 'Don't ask me.'

Encouraged by Sourmuddle, twittered at by Sharkadder and prodded firmly by Macabre, Scott finally consented to mount the podium. Spectators hurried back to their seats, consulting their programmes, adjusting their binoculars, taking up their flags and finishing off their sandwiches. Filth began a little drum roll, then stopped when he saw Sourmuddle glaring and shaking her head. Apparently, they weren't quite ready.

Aware that all eyes were upon him, Scott slipped into professional superstar mode. He clicked open his briefcase and removed a sheaf of papers. Sharkadder came rushing up with his glass of water, then scuttled away to join the Witch team.

Scott waited until all the coughs died down. The spellovision crew moved in for a close-up. Taking his time, he arranged his papers, then took up the megaphone that Pongwiffy had thoughtfully supplied. He took a deep breath, then his sonorous voice rolled around the stadium.

'Friends,' said Scott. 'My very good friends. You all know me. Scott Sinister, the famous star of stage and screen, who has condescended to come here today and be your commentator. What's more, I'm doing it for free.'

He paused for applause, which dutifully came. He flashed his sunglasses, smiled for the camera and added, 'By the way, I've got a new film coming out, so fans, take note. But enough about me. I've got a job to do.' His voice became solemn. 'We are gathered here together on this glorious morn for an historic occasion. A momentous occasion. An occasion which, in a long line of occasions, stands out as the occasion which . . .'

'Get on with it!' shouted a cheeky Gnome in the front row. He wasn't a fan.

'As I was saying,' continued Scott, glaring at the heckler. 'An occasion which is probably the best occasion Witchway Wood has ever had. *The O'Lumpicks!*'

He threw up his arms, and the place exploded with thunderous clapping and ringing cheers.

'Yes!' cried Scott emotionally. 'Yes! Raise your voices! Let's hear it for the very first Witchway Wood O'Lumpick Games!'

'Hooray!' screamed the crowds, leaping on seats and waving flags.

'Fitness!' cried Scott. 'Health, fitness and dedication. That's what the O'Lumpicks are all about.'

'And shorts!' someone shouted.

'Yes! And shorts. And noble participation. And a lot of other stuff, but enough of that. We want to move on, don't we? The Games must commence! For your delight and amazement, we begin with a Grand Opening Parade . . .'

'Not yet,' hissed Sourmuddle from the sidelines.

'What?'

'Keep talking. We're not ready to start.'

'Eh? Why not?'

'Pongwiffy hasn't arrived. She leads us in.'

Scott frowned. He hadn't prepared for this. He liked to stick to a script. Improvisation wasn't his strong point. But the audience was getting restless. The spellovision camera was trained on him and he had to say something.

'Ahem. Before we start the Parade, just a bit more about me. Not everyone knows this, but as well as an actor I'm a bit of a poet in my spare time. You'll be amazed to hear I've written my commentary in poetic verse. Now, I don't know if any of you have ever tried this, but it's not easy. Finding the right rhyme takes a lot of effort. For

192

instance, nothing rhymes with *orange*. There are many other words which prove difficult. *Juggernaut*, for example. *Palaeanthropological*. *Zigzag*, that's a hard one. Um . . . *rhubarb* . . .'

*   *   *

Back at *Sugary Candy's*, it was a very different scene. Philpot lay in a sticky heap on the floor. His face was covered in chocolate and streaked with multicoloured trails of encrusted dribble. He was a total mess—and blissfully happy. Together, he and his new friend had eaten their way through enough sweets and chocolate to sink a barge.

Philpot felt great, but his new friend wasn't looking so good. She was stretched out on the counter, eyes tightly shut, groaning and looking green. Philpot heaved himself into a sitting position. It took some effort because he was lying on a heap of melted toffee and his back was stuck to the floor.

'WALKIES?' said Philpot brightly, reaching up and patting her on the cheek with a revoltingly sticky hand.

'What?' moaned Pongwiffy. With an effort, she sat up. 'Oooh. Where am I? What's happening? What time is it?'

Groggily, she looked around. Bright sunlight poured through the broken window. It made her head ache.

Wait a minute. Sunlight? When she had first entered the shop, the sun hadn't even risen properly. Could she have dropped off for a minute or two? In between finishing off the jar of *Gloopy Guzzlers* and getting stuck in to the *Minty*

Stingeroos? It was all a bit of a blur. Something niggled at the back of her mind, though. She was supposed to *be* somewhere. There was something very important that—

Oh. Oh dear. Oh deary deary dear. In fact— *arrrrrrrgh!*

CHAPTER TWENTY-THREE

LATE AGAIN

'. . . and then there's *garlic*,' Scott told the puzzled crowd. 'That's a tricky one. And *spontaneous*. I'd defy anyone to find a rhyme for that. Anyone know a word that rhymes with *spontaneous*?' Deafening silence greeted this. 'No? I thought not.'

He took out a large white hanky and mopped his brow. He was feeling faint and his mouth was horribly dry, unlike the rest of him, which was bathed in perspiration.

'Keep going,' hissed Sourmuddle.

'I'm not sure I can,' croaked Scott. 'I'm losing my voice.'

'You're losing their interest too,' said Sourmuddle. 'Say something different before they start throwing things.'

She was right. The crowds were clearly getting bored with being lectured about poetry. They wanted the Grand Opening Parade. Someone started a slow hand clap, which was taken up with enthusiasm by athletes and supporters alike.

Scott reached out a trembling hand and took another swig from his water glass. He didn't think he could go on. His mind was blank. Not only could he not think of any more words that didn't rhyme with any other words, he couldn't think of any words *at all*. He had done what all actors dread. He had dried up.

And then he was saved. All heads turned as the palace gates opened with a loud clang, and a familiar, dishevelled figure stood framed in the gap. She had lost her hat and was panting heavily.

The slow clapping died away. A breeze blew. Somebody coughed.

Grandwitch Sourmuddle said nothing. She simply beckoned with a single curling finger.

Poor Pongwiffy. It was a horrible moment.

She set off on the long walk. The spellovision camera swivelled, capturing her every move. After what seemed like a week, she arrived at the podium.

'*Late*,' said Sourmuddle. 'Embarrassingly, ludicrously, unbelievably *late*.'

'Mmm . . . yes,' agreed Pongwiffy, adding rather feebly, 'Sorry.'

'*Why?*'

'Fell out of bed, banged my head, unconscious for hours,' explained Pongwiffy, and immediately came out in the pesky green spots. So everyone knew she was fibbing.

'Oooh,' muttered the crowd disapprovingly. 'Fibber.'

'*Spots*,' snapped Sourmuddle. 'Try again.'

'Lost my memory?'

'No, you didn't. Tell me another one.'

196

'Kidnapped by pirates?'

'*More* spots. Getting really bad now,' said Sourmuddle. 'Let's see how long before they all join up and you become one big green boil. I'm rather enjoying this. *Do* keep going.'

The entire watching arena nodded. Sport could wait. The Grand Opening Parade could wait. Watching Pongwiffy try to wriggle her way out of this one would provide a whole new world of entertainment. It certainly made a change from poetry.

Pongwiffy took a deep breath. There was nothing else for it. She would have to tell the truth. After all, this was the O'Lumpicks. They were supposed to be noble and truthful and fair. You shouldn't really tell fibs on a day like this.

'Well,' she said. 'Here's the truth. There's a wild Giant baby loose in the Wood. I saw him. He's broken the window of *Sugary Candy's*. He's in there scoffing free sweets. I've been trying to drive him off, and that's why I'm late. If you don't believe me, go and look for yourselves.'

It wasn't entirely a lie, although Pongwiffy can't resist an embellishment and it still veered slightly from the absolute truth. The spots subsided a little.

From all around came a muttering. The muttering grew to a grumbling. Little conversations were breaking out. What was this? The unbreakable, magically fortified, impregnable window of *Sugary Candy's* had finally given way?

There were free sweets?

Sweets. Ooh, that word! It leapt out from the sentence, overshadowing anything that had gone before, including even interesting words such as

197

wild, Giant, baby and loose in the Wood. *Sweets*. That was the important word, the one that everyone heard, the one they fixated on. And it brought back such memories. Memories of what it was like going to *Sugary Candy's* before the O'Lumpicks took over. The fun. The anticipation in the queue. Drooling over the labels, wondering what to buy. Placing the order. Parting with your life savings. Coming away with a thousand crackling packages of gooey stickiness. Hurrying home, switching on the spello and diving in!

Everyone forgot the bad things, of course. How you always felt sick in the end. The tooth troubles. The spots, the flabby tummies, the lack of get-up-and-go, the sheer expense. All they remembered was the wonderful, glorious, utterly all-consuming *taste*.

There was a collective intake of breath. A sort of vast, communal, gasping sigh.

And then . . .

STAMPEEEEEEEEDE!!!

The audience rocketed from their seats and, as one, charged for the gates. And not only the audience. The podium rocked threateningly as hordes of well-honed, treat-starved teams of athletes surged past, all thoughts of health, fitness, intermingling, sportsmanship, games, medals and even shorts abandoned. Replaced by a single, primal thought.

Sweets!

Within a matter of moments, Pongwiffy was alone in an empty garden. Well, alone apart from King Futtout, who was unsuccessfully trying to untangle himself from his throne, which had been unceremoniously overturned by the mob. And

Scott Sinister.

'Well,' said Scott after a long silence. He gathered up his carefully composed verses and placed them in his briefcase, which he closed with a sharp little click. 'I take it my services are no longer required.'

'Looks like it,' said Pongwiffy sadly.

'Yet again, all ends in chaos.'

'Yep.'

'I won't say *I told you so*,' said Scott bitterly. 'I won't say *I knew it*. I won't say your wretched O'Lumpicks are clearly an unmitigated disaster and it's *all your fault.*'

'No,' agreed Pongwiffy. 'Probably not a good idea to say those things right now.'

'I'll be off, then,' said Scott. Very deliberately, he dropped his megaphone on to the podium and stamped on it. It splintered into a thousand small pieces.

Then he stepped down from the podium and paused. 'One last thing. Don't ask me for any more favours. *Ever* again.'

Pongwiffy watched him stalk off, picking his way between broken flags, torn banners, forgotten picnic baskets, hats, vibrant cloaks, odd shoes, a cabbage, trampled carrots and other abandoned items.

'Hey!' shouted Pongwiffy as he strode through the gates. She had just thought of something. 'What about my special poem? I know you've written one, Hugo told me!'

What Scott said was short, sharp and luckily unintelligible. You could tell it was rude, though.

There came the sound of a coach moving off at high speed—and he was gone.

That was that, then.

Slowly, Pongwiffy sat down on the edge of the podium. She felt—crushed. After all that effort, everything she had worked for had come to nothing. There would be no flag bearing. No Grand Opening Parade. No Games. No one would ever intermingle. No medals would be won. The dream was over.

And to crown it all, she had given in and pigged out on sweets, after all the effort she'd put into getting fit.

Of course, she wasn't alone. By now, she had no doubts that everyone was swarming over *Sugary Candy's* like ants on a sugar mountain, fighting over the best stuff, filling their hats and pockets and cramming their mouths like there was no tomorrow.

But she of all people should have been stronger. Or at least kept her mouth shut and said nothing. At the next Coven Meeting there would be Big Trouble. Sourmuddle would order an inquiry. She would get blamed for everything, as usual. Nothing had changed. She was still the same old Pongwiffy.

'But fitter,' said a voice at her elbow. Hugo was sitting next to her, little legs swinging.

'Oh, it's you,' muttered Pongwiffy. 'What did you say?' She hadn't realised she had spoken out loud.

'Still same but fitter.'

Pongwiffy shrugged. Somehow, without the spur of the O'Lumpicks, the whole fitness thing had lost its charm. She didn't care any more.

'You OK?' said Hugo. Pongwiffy didn't go in for silence often. It wasn't her style.

'I've been better,' she said.

'Lost your hat?'

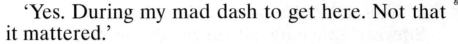

'Yes. During my mad dash to get here. Not that it mattered.'

'Is true about wild Giant baby?'

'Yes. I said, didn't I?'

'You try to drive wild Giant baby out of sweet shop? All by yourself?'

'Yes. *Yes*, all right?' The spots returned, but Hugo didn't mention it.

'I help you find hat later.'

'Thanks.'

There was a little silence. Together, they watched King Futtout finally disentangle himself from his throne and wander off towards the palace, clutching his box of unwanted medals and moaning a bit. A footman came running out and led him away.

'He voulda been rubbish judge anyway,' said Hugo.

'He would,' agreed Pongwiffy. 'Too scared to say who's won. No powers of decision.'

'Big royal scaredy cat.'

'Don't know why we chose him.'

'Zoze medals!' Hugo gave a sneer. 'You see zem? Ze pits. Nobody vant vun, I sink. Not me, not you, not no vun.'

Pongwiffy fumbled in her pocket and brought out a handful of fluff-covered *Hoppy Jumpers*. They were all stuck together. They didn't look appetising.

'Want one?' she said.

'Sure,' said Hugo. He selected the least fluffy and popped it in his mouth. Pongwiffy stared down at the rest, shrugged, then crammed them in her mouth.

'By the way,' she said indistinctly. 'I never did

ask. Who was doing what in your team?'

'Me on ze Veights. Dudley on ze Sack Race, Barry and Speks on ze Three-Legged, Rory on ze High Jump, Vernon on ze Egg and Spoon, nobody Tossink ze Caber, Steve and IdentiKit and CopiCat and ze fastest Bat on ze Relay.'

'I'd like to have seen Rory doing the High Jump,' said Pongwiffy.

'Me too.'

'I wonder how Steve would have coped with the baton? In the Relay? Swallowed it or something?'

'Wound himself round it and rolled,' said Hugo. 'I see him practise. He voz gettink quite good. I sink maybe ve vin zat.'

'Maybe. It doesn't matter now though, does it?'

Together, they sat quietly chewing, staring around the deserted stadium. It was quite nice really. Peaceful. Companionable. The calm after the storm.

And then Philpot arrived.

CHAPTER TWENTY-FOUR

PHILPOT'S JOURNEY

You may be wondering what happened to Philpot after Pongwiffy shot out of his life without so much as a goodbye. Well, it's quite simple. He followed her.

For once in his short life, Philpot had eaten enough. Being weaned on a diet of pretend medicine, he had a cast-iron stomach. He had tried everything that *Sugary Candy's* had to offer. Together, more or less silently, he and his new friend had raided every jar—crunching, slurping, chewing and generally sampling everything except for the blinking eyeballs.

All that gorging meant that Philpot was full to bursting. The spilled mountains and open jars held no more secrets. He was all done with eating, bursting with energy and more than ready for something new.

Finding himself suddenly alone and abandoned,

he decided to see where his new friend had gone. Perhaps she was around the corner, hiding behind a tree, waiting to play peek-a-boo with him, like Nana Su-Su. Or even better, Hide and Seek. His eyes sparkled at the thought. He missed Nana Su-Su. He wished she was here now. But she wasn't, so his new, smelly friend with the pointy head would have to do.

Trailing his leash, he waded across the sticky, glass-strewn floor and stepped out into the sunshine.

There was no sign of his new friend. She must be hiding. Ooh, what fun, he would find her.

Giggling hopefully, he set off along the trail.

We won't bother to go into detail here. Philpot's journey is not that interesting. It goes in fits and starts and it takes a while. He fell down and cried once or twice. A bush scratched him. He saw a stone he liked but got bored with carrying it. At one point, he found a stick and waved it around a bit. Then he remembered his new friend and toddled on.

You may be wondering how he knew which way to go. It was the smell. Simple as that. Pongwiffy is nothing if not easy to trace.

At one point, Philpot found her hat. He picked it up and tried it on, but it was too small so he dropped it in the mud and stepped on it before moving on.

And so it went on.

The main event in Philpot's journey was probably the mob. He was quite surprised when he came face to face with that. He wasn't expecting a rampaging *mob* to come charging at him at all. He stood his ground, though. He stood swaying on his

204

tree trunk legs, frowning a bit, waiting to see what the mob would do. He might be only a baby, but he was a big one.

The mob consisted of a motley assortment of Witches, Skeletons, Trolls—oh, you know who they were. It may interest you to hear that the faddy Werewolf was in the lead, closely challenged by Gaga, although Sourmuddle had a surprisingly fair turn of speed, as did Rory. Overhead was a collection of flying things, some of whose names we know.

The mob didn't even attempt to mow Philpot down. They just neatly parted and ran straight past him, like water round a boulder. So what if there was a Giant baby loose in the Wood? They'd think about that later. There were free sweets!

The howls died away, the dust settled and Philpot moved on.

In time, the trees thinned out. Ahead of him was something new. A high wall. Beyond the wall, he could see pretty flags fluttering in the breeze. There were gates in the wall and they stood wide open. In fact, one of them hung off its hinges.

Philpot's eyes widened. What adventures lay beyond?

He knew one thing. That was where his new friend had gone.

*   *   *

'Well, would you look at that,' said Pongwiffy to Hugo. 'If it's not the Giant baby. That's all we need.'

Hugo stared. There was certainly a Giant baby. He could see that. Philpot was hard to miss.

'Vill it attack?' he whispered cautiously.

'No. I'm afraid it rather likes me. Don't move, perhaps it won't notice us.'

The pair of them watched to see what Philpot would do. He stared around, thumb in mouth, observing the overturned chairs, the smashed spellovision camera, the thousand and one scattered items left behind in the mass exodus. None of it made any sense to him. Then he caught sight of Pongwiffy. He broke into a delighted grin.

At last! His new friend! Found her!

'GA!' he bellowed triumphantly. 'GA! GA!'

And he came lumbering unsteadily across the lawn, arms outstretched in happy greeting.

'Oh bother, it's spotted me,' said Pongwiffy tiredly. 'I suppose this'll be something *else* I have to worry about.'

But just then, something unexpected happened. There came a shout from the gates.

'Baby Philpot! *Dere* you is!'

Philpot froze in mid-toddle. He knew that voice. He turned around. An even bigger grin split his fat pink face in two.

'NANA SU-SU!'

The two of them ran towards each other. You can add slow motion here if you like, but it's not necessary. At any rate, their reunion was emotional. There was a lot of smiling through tears.

'Hugo,' said Pongwiffy slowly. 'Am I dreaming, or is that Plugugly in a *dress*? Wearing a—*flowery bonnet*?'

'Ya,' said Hugo. 'It is. And look! More of zem!' He pointed to the gates, where the rest of the Gaggle were skulking nervously, clearly too frightened to enter.

'*Goblins*?' Pongwiffy was outraged. 'The whole Gaggle? Here? In *broad daylight*? Are they *mad*? If this doesn't call for a zapping, I don't know what does.'

'Ze brazen cheek of it!' cried Hugo. 'You vant I bite zeir ankles, get rid of zem? Just say ze vord!'

'No, hang on. I want to know what's happening. Why is Plugugly dressed like that? And why is he hugging the baby's leg in that ridiculous way?'

In the very centre of the arena, Plugugly was indeed hugging Philpot's leg. It was one of the few remaining bits of Philpot he could get his arms around. Philpot had expanded even more since the last time they were together. The leg felt unpleasantly sticky, as though he'd been rolling in something. But Plugugly was brimful of joy to see him. It was such a relief to find him safe and sound.

Philpot was delighted to be reunited with Nanny Susan too. He was chuckling with glee and trying to crawl into Plugugly's arms, which in effect meant knocking him over. Plugugly didn't mind one bit.

It would be nice to linger on this tender scene. But then . . .

VROOOOOOOOMMMMMM!

There was a great, thunderous, roaring noise. Through the palace gates came a massive, shiny red motorbike!

The Stonkings had returned from Giant Town!

The visit had been a partial success. Largette had gone shopping and bought some lovely shoes. Bigsy had had a tattoo done. It was across his stomach and said BABY PHILPO (the tattooist had run out of ink). The two of them had eaten well, gone dancing and caught up with old friends. The family barbecue hadn't gone too brilliantly, however. It had ended in a squabble, which is a shame.

On the whole, though, it had been a nice break. They were back now, and eager to be reunited with Baby Philpot. Had they missed him? Not a lot. But they were very keen to see if he had grown much. Besides, Largette had bought him a big blue bib, in preparation for that exciting day when he went on to solids.

How did they know that Philpot was to be found in the palace grounds, you may wonder. Had their way home taken them past *Sugary Candy's*? Had they overheard one of the ransacking mob talking about a Giant baby, in between hoovering up sweets? Or had they just driven past and spotted him by accident? Nobody knows. All that matters is that they are here.

The giant bike raced past the Gaggle, who scattered. It roared through the gates and across the lawn, which was already badly churned up. It came to a screeching halt right in the middle, where Plugugly and Philpot were still hugging each other.

Bigsy turned off the engine. Largette planted a red high heel on the lawn and dismounted.

Over on the podium, Pongwiffy and Hugo watched the proceedings with drop-jawed disbelief. For once, they were speechless. They were used to strange things happening in Witchway Wood, it was that kind of place. But this was seriously weird. A Giant baby was one thing, but a couple of full-sized Giants arriving from nowhere on a blooming great giant motorbike was a step too far.

For a moment, nothing happened. Plugugly stared at the Stonkings and the Stonkings stared at Plugugly. Then they stared at their baby.

Their baby was a baby no more. He was a proper toddler. He was unbelievably filthy. He was clearly massively sticky. He was HUGE. My oh my, had he grown. Was this the same child they had left behind?

Philpot broke the spell. He stared shyly up at the two strangers, held up his chubby arms and said really sweetly, 'MAMA? DADA?'

Largette burst into tears and Bigsy fell to his knees and scooped Philpot into his arms.

He was absolutely perfect. They loved him!

Over on the podium, Pongwiffy and Hugo continued to watch the bewildering scene that was unravelling before their eyes.

What was this? Plugugly talking to Giants? Laughter, even? A lot of hugging and kissing and baby throwing? A large bag of gold being taken from a saddlebag and deposited in Plugugly's eager arms? More talk and happy laughter? Fond farewells? The Giants roaring off on the bike with the baby perched dangerously on the female's shoulders, screeching his delight to the wind?

And Plugugly's reaction when they had gone. That was worth observing. The short, noisy weep into the apron, followed by the instant cheering up when he suddenly remembered what he was holding.

They watched him pick up his skirts and race towards the rest of the Gaggle, who had regrouped at the gates, looking impatient. There was a brief exchange of words, and then they were gone.

That was it. Drama over. Once again it was back to a deserted stadium. Pongwiffy and Hugo were alone again.

'Well,' said Pongwiffy after a bit, 'I wonder what all that was about?'

CHAPTER TWENTY-FIVE

WHAT YOU MAY WANT
TO KNOW

For those of you who like to have everything neatly
tied up, here is a short summary.

RONALD

For Ronald, just like everyone else, the prospect of
free sweets had proved irresistible. He had raced
off with the mob, intent on getting there first and
helping himself to the best ones. Sadly, he got
knocked over and trampled on by a Zombie en
route. Then his shorts elastic gave way and he had
to slow down and walk, which meant that he was
the last to arrive.

Sharkadder spotted him as he came shuffling
into *Sugary Candy's*. She had her long arm stuck
into a jar of *Bat Splatz* at the time. But that didn't
stop her eagle eye from noticing a suspicious-

213

looking spoon handle protruding from his pocket. A single barked command later and a red-faced Ronald was forced to disclose his shocking secret to the world. He was revealed as a sneaky cheat in front of everybody. Although it has to be said that nobody cared that much, because the O'Lumpicks were now over—well, they would never *begin*, put it like that—and the rules regarding sportsmanship no longer applied. It was back to the old ways, with every man for himself. Besides, they were all too busy scoffing sweets.

Ronald got punished, though. He got a strong lecture from Sharkadder. She wouldn't let him take any sweets either. He was sent back to the Clubhouse in disgrace, expecting another telling-off when he got home.

Luckily for him, his fellow Wizards never even knew that he had applied. They had forgotten that the O'Lumpicks were on and were watching something really boring on the other channel. So it could have been worse.

KING FUTTOUT

It took him several days to recover and many long weeks to set his garden back in order. He got it in the neck from Queen Beryl and Princess Honeydimple too, when they finally returned laden with dresses, handbags and shoes. Queen Beryl made him write a letter of complaint to Grandwitch Sourmuddle, and sent a footman to post it this time.

He didn't even get a reply.

SCOTT

Like the trouper he is, Scott put the experience behind him and moved on. He made a small bonfire of his poems, then went off to start rehearsing for his next film, which is currently doing good business at the box office. It has yet to be seen by Pongwiffy, although Hugo says it's good. It's called *Dark Night of the Mad Mutant Horror Hamsters*, so he would say that.

THE YETIS

They weren't too happy about things, particularly when they saw the state of their lovely shop, even though they hadn't exactly been paying it much attention since putting the notice on the door. They decided to abandon the whole project and go back to what they did best—kebab stalls, pizza parlours and greasy spoon joints. Although Spag is wondering whether an ice-cream parlour in Witchway Wood might catch on. They are currently away in the Antarctic, looking for a source of cheap ice.

*   *   *

THE GOBLINS

You will be interested to know that the Goblins finally made it to *Sugary Candy's*, armed with their bag of gold. Sadly, the mob had got there before them. When they finally showed up, there wasn't a single thing left. The place had been swept clean, apart from the untouched jar of blinking eyeballs.

But Goblins will eat anything. They fell upon the

jar, wrenched off the top and got stuck in. While they were thus occupied, someone stole the bag of gold, which was a shame. They never did find out who.

Plugugly kept the dress. He still tries it on from time to time, in memory of Baby Philpot. Even though the others jeer at him.

THE STONKINGS

They moved back to Giant Town, taking Philpot with them. He is the apple of their eye and both his grandmas adore him. He is the centre of attention at family barbecues, is growing bigger every day and can say whole sentences now. He has forgotten Nanny Susan.

So there you have it. You know what happened to everyone. Except Pongwiffy. Perhaps we'll pop into Number One, Dump Edge, one last time, to see how she's doing.

A week has gone by since we last saw her. Right now, she is sitting at the table, banging a fork and waiting for supper. Outside, night is falling and the stars are out.

'You know what I'm sorry about, Hugo?' said Pongwiffy.

'No. Vot?'

'I'm sorry I never got to hear Scott's poem. The one about me.'

'Mmm,' said Hugo.

'I wonder how it went? Sharkadder's pretending she's forgotten. I don't suppose Dudley said, did he?'

'No,' said Hugo quickly. 'Not a vord.'

He was being kind here. In fact, Dudley had repeated it to him, word for word. It went like this.

A word of thanks I'm forced to say
To she who organised this day.
She worked quite hard to sort it out
Of that I do not have a doubt.
We should have given her a prize
But we forgot, surprise, surprise.
I end now with a final plea.
Pongwiffy, stay away from me!
Do not visit, write or call.
I do not like you, not at all.

'Oh well,' said Pongwiffy. 'Perhaps it's just as well. I don't want to get big-headed.'

'Mmm.'

'And at least the O'Lumpicks weren't a *complete* waste of time. Everyone enjoyed the race to the sweet shop. And they all keep coming up and telling me how much fitter they feel these days and how they're going to keep eating healthy stuff and carry on working out. So am I actually. In fact, I'm quite looking forward to the Coven Meeting tonight. We're flying to Crag Hill, did you know? For the exercise. Get *down*, Broom, not yet. Come on, Hugo, I'm hungry. What's for supper?'

'Skunk stew,' said Hugo. 'Your favourite. I make special.'

'Really? Well, that's very nice of you. I won't have too much, mustn't be greedy.'

In the event, though, she was very greedy indeed and had three platefuls.

But—and this is important—with a healthy dish of peas on the side.

217